THE CHINESE RAPPER

Jeff Crowder

Amazon

ISBN-13: 9798840735510
ISBN-10:

Cover design by: Art Painter
Library of Congress Control Number: 2018675309
Printed in the United States of America

CONTENTS

CHAPTER 1

The first time I ever met the Chinese Rapper was in July of 2006, about a year after hurricane Katrina wreaked havoc on the Louisiana coast. I was a bartender at the Shanghai Sushi Lounge in Austin Texas. He was scheduled to give a performance and when I heard his name, I almost busted out laughing. I have to admit though, the guy was pretty good. So good I decided to record his following performances to document his songs for all eternity even though some of them sucked. The funny thing was he managed to attract hecklers. One in particular used to try to interrupt him so much he incorporated the guy in some of his songs. This heckler was a big, old cowboy that was perpetually perturbed by this young man. It was kind of funny to watch these two interact with each other and it provided some comical entertainment for the folks fortunate, or unfortunate enough, depending how you looked at it, to witness this odd relationship.

I tried to arrange them in his original order as I heard them even though I'm sure he wouldn't approve of my revelations of his songs, I felt it was important to at least try to keep them in some sort of timeline. This first one blew me away since it was about the hurricane that changed so many lives and caused so much controversy. He seemed to have inside knowledge of the event that changed history forever down here in my neck of the woods. The cowboy got pissed off and started giving him a big raft of shit near the end of his song which seemed to agree with many of the drunken patrons at the time. I wish you could've been there. He used typical rap beats for his unique numbers that seemed to jive in such a way that impressed me, and I witnessed many lounge acts in my days. He named the first one The Truth even though I somehow doubt that's what it was.

The Truth

"This is the track where I expose the truth.
Don't mind the fish bone stuck in my tooth.
The Louisiana dyke explosion was a thought-out plan.
To flood the poor people, not the rich man.
A boy from Texas was hired to do the job.
His boss said, boy, pull that out of your ass, that stupid corncob.
You have to go to New Orleans with a demolition team.
Leave your rubber dolly at home, and don't bring your cream.
This has to be a secret so keep your mouth shut.
If Spike Lee tries to find you, kick him in the butt.
Do you know what I'm saying?
Plant the time bombs and put the dynamite all-around.
The cops found it too late and blew up Hector the bomb sniffing hound.
The hurricane destroyed all the evidence.
But pieces of Hector were found at the mayor's residence.
That dumb doggy. His death had cops feeling froggy.
The Texas cowboy bomber started to run away.
He got away from angry residents yelling, why don't you stay?
He was running down the beach and got hit by Katrina.
Woke up in the swamp with some Cajun boy, he's never seen anyone meaner.
He told the Cajun what he did, and he started to laugh.
He said, now boy George will have to fire his whole staff.
Oh! Then he let him go after threatening to feed him to the gators.
By sundown he was at home eating mommy's rotten taters.
She said, Samuel Hall, where on earth did you go?
He spit a tobacco wad, let out a burp, and said, I don't know.
The lard ass seen him on the news running away.
She said, I'm your big, fat mama, here it's safe to stay.
Ha! Ha! Ha! American hunk of trash. Ha! Ha! Ha!

Watch out for the hurricane. Oh!
Sorry, he didn't mean to blow up that piece of garbage.
He didn't mean to flood out Louisiana.
But he did it wearing a hair piece and a hippy's bandana.
He had to get the hell out of that flooded place.
Oh! They were going to shoot him in the face.
Bang! Bang! Bang! But he got away.
He went to Texas and that's where he stays.
His mama's an two-timing, ugly, fat whore.
She couldn't even fit through the kitchen door.
They dined on the fine cuisine of fish heads and rice.
She said, boy, if you don't do it right the first time, I'll make you do
it twice.
So, he did the job correctly and did it good.
He did what in his heart he knew a good boy should.
Boy George went berzerk and ultimately crazy.
FEMA turned out to be inadequite and somewhat lazy.
A lot of poor people died and their mama's cried.
That's why I'm going to whip boy George's hide.
With a leather belt and a whip.
I'll say, man, you turned out to be a dip.
Why did I vote for the other man?
You stole the election at your brother's hand.
You know you're going to be shot.
You'll be 6 feet under, and your bones will rot.
Bang! Bang! Bang!
His whiz kid contemporary has been up to no good.
When I kill him, I'm going to wear a long black hood.
So, the CIA won't catch me.
I'm a Chinese spy and I will flee.
Back to China, my homeland.
We took over your foreign land.
Boy George gave up the whole country.
Then he came to China and planted a tree.
In memory of all those that passed away.
And all the people that turned gay.

Ugh! I forgot to call FEMA, I'm no master sleuth.

Now you know every inch of the unvarnished truth," he sang with all the showmanship he could muster.

This was when the cowboy spoke up, and more or less admitted his role in the conspiracy. He seemed madder than hell as he confronted the Chinese Rapper right after his strange song. I transcribed it word for word, but I guess you had to be there to witness this weird exchange.

"They never spotted me hiding in the nearby bushes," he said and then went into a diabolical song of his own.

"I killed a man they said, so they said. I killed a man they said, and I smashed in his head. And I left him lying dead, and said, blast his hide."

The Chinese rapper tried to continue his song but was cut off again after a couple lines.

"The masses were shocked and appalled by my truthful revelation. I reorganized the chaos into a manageable variation," he sang as he tried to continue but was cut off by the drunken cowboy.

"I did what I was supposed to. For my boss you know. That farm boy with the big, old cowboy hat. Hell, we went into the restaurant and had some beans and some cornbread. Anyhow, he told me he'd give me 1000 bucks to go to Louisiana," he bellowed and then continued.

"I said, I'll go to Louisiana, I'll blow up them dikes. I hope nobody gets hurt, but you know I'll blow them up. Because, hell, the hurricane was coming, and I knew that. Well, I blew them up with Nitro and TNT. A bunch of, all kinds of stuff, you know. I used a little fertilizer on them suckers. Put a little timebomb on her. I had it timed just right, right when the hurricane was coming. I hope nobody floats over those bombs. They're powerful enough to blow sky high, somebody's face. I hope nobody drifted over those bombs. They would definitely blow somebody's head off," he said blowing away the small audience leaving them speechless with half their mouths gaping.

The Chinese Rapper was poised to continue but the

cowboy wouldn't remain silent as he continued with his strange revelation.

"I saw it with my own two eyes, I was chewing tobacco, I spit out a wad. And then I looked over and there it was, the hurricane. And then there it was, a giant explosion. I didn't know what happened, but I saw some boy from Texas run away from the scene. I said, I'll trade that gallon in your hand for a two-dollar bill, you little Texas boy. I heard the hurricane and then I turned around and looked. I drank me some booze, and I turned around and looked. And I said, 'what the heck, it looks like an explosion.'"

People in the bar were shocked but the Chinese Rapper was getting pissed. This rodeo clown stole the show, and the Chinese Rapper was visibly perturbed as the cowboy kept rolling on with his strange confession.

"Yes sir! I saw a giant explosion. I just think we're all going to die," he said.

Another patron there that night stood up and seemed to contradict the boisterous fellow and seemed to know who he was. Talk about a strange confrontation. The Chinese Rapper just stood there, with his hands on his hips in disgust, and the other customers watched in shock as these two argued.

"I recognized him. I tried to fire this guy. He filed a complaint against me," said the businessman looking gentleman.

"Yeah! That's because he tried to kill me. He tried to give me duck flu," the cowboy retorted.

"He said he felt threatened in the workplace."

"That's because I got my ass kicked everyday by Chinese immigrants."

"So then, ultimately, they fired him, because he showed up to work drunk," said the businessman which the crowd naturally agreed was true by the looks of the cowboy drunk ruining their Saturday night show.

That's when the Chinese Rapper interjected, "They were trying to beat up a Chinese boy. I had to show them some xiung xiu," he said making karate chop motions to much laughter, embarrassing the loudmouth cowboy.

"Stay away from this Chinese guy, he will hurt you bad boy," said the businessman to the cowboy motioning to the Chinese singer which made the crowd erupt in cheers.

"I will xiung xiu your face so bad you'll be sorry you were ever born," said the rapper.

"He said I was a barbarian to work for," said the businessman as he sat back down.

"Yeah! That's because he dressed up in leather and whipped me with his belt every morning," said the cowboy as people were trying to get him to shut up, but he went on.

"I've been watching those dikes since I was a little boy. I never seen an explosion like that. That was enough to blow sky high somebody's face. I'm so glad I wasn't standing over those bombs. That Spike Lee sure got it on the head when he said that it blew up," he said as people started booing his interruptions which brought a smile to the face of the Chinese Rapper.

"I went to Louisiana looking for some beans. But they didn't have any. I blew that boys shit away because he didn't have any beans. He smelled them beans and got the hell out of Dodge. The police can't tell us exactly who he is," he tried to say but was interrupted himself.

"He's a patsy for the Louisiana dike explosion," someone yelled in the bar causing hearty laughter from the crowd.

"They forced him to drive to a deserted area. Once there, they kicked the man out and stole his car," said the businessman.

"XFJ007, I guess I better change my license plate if I want some beans from Texas," said the singer causing the crowd and even me to laugh.

"He ate a bunch of beans and blew out the courtroom," said the cowboy getting booed but he kept on. "That old boy didn't have any beans. I like them Texas beans boy. See, I was born in Texas. I was chewing tobacco one day and I spit out a wad. And all of a sudden here come this old boy, and he said, 'guess what? You know the Louisiana dike explosion, have you ever heard of that?'

"No, I haven't heard of that," spoke up the Chinese Rapper causing a few smiles.

"Well, they're trying to say someone blew up the dikes. Some old boy blew up the dikes on purpose, and they said it was you. I offered him two dollars for his 10-gallon hat."

"Sit down and shut up!" somebody yelled but he went on.

"And he said, I'm going to shoot some beechnut in your eyeball, and pop your nose out and fart in it. And I have the worst farts imaginable because I've been eating those Texas beans since the day I was born. Right out of the can. I don't cook them or nothing, they're just raw beans. And I mean I mix them with my chewing tobacco when I'm eating. Then I swallow them beans and that old chew kind of burns. It will rip roar your nose right in two. It'll curl your nostril hairs," the cowboy informed the crowd.

"Go back up north you pansy. Don't mess with Texas," some heckler said to the heckling cowboy.

He said, "I'll mess with Texas anytime I want to, you little weasel," to the unknown patron.

"Kick the crap off your boots, you redneck piece of garbage," the man in the crowd said.

"You fat piece of crap. You look like some kind of a piece of toiletry that came off some rotten Winnebago that's been sitting in some crappy RV Park in Waco," the cowboy said.
At this point many in the crowd were getting up to leave which pissed me off because that would be cutting into my tips for the night.

"I hope I'll be forgiven for this because it was a necessary assignment," said the Chinese Rapper implying that he was the one that did it in a vain attempt to reel the exiting crowds back in.

"Don't tell me you cut down the motherland, Texas," the cowboy continued arguing with the man in the crowd.

"That's where my mama was born and raised. When you're cutting down Texas, you're cutting down the chewing tobacco factory., you're cutting down the bean farm, and you're cutting down me."

"Go back up north, you piece of bean eating little. Piece of bean eating little, Piece of bean eating little, piece of fart," spoke up the businessman getting flustered.

"Is that all you could call me was a piece of fart? I call you a piece of crap, with beans in it, and corn, and everything else. Because you looked like a fool when you were born. Your mama looked down and seen the evil in your devilish eyes," retorted the cowboy at which point the Chinese Rapper rejoined.

"I said, yeah, it's got beady eyes, it's got eyes from Texas. I said, spit out that tobacco, you little baby. I said, here you go, here's your cowboy hat and your six-shooter. You little piece of crap. Go back to Texas," said the singer on his mic overpowering the voice of the cowboy which made him yell even louder.

"Well guess what? I could kick your ass any day of the week. I'll just put in a big wad of tobacco and punch you in the eye. I'll be happy to give you a big, Texas sized black eye."

"Go ahead, you bean eating little cowboy with your 10-gallon hat. And your six-shooting little piece of garbage, cap gun or whatever you call it. Oh, man, those spurs on your cowboy boots jingling. What do you use those boots for? To kick the donkey in the butt when he won't move? Or to give your old lady some Texas style donkey loving?" The rapper said making the crowd laugh.

"I tell you what I'm going to do. As soon as I chew my tobacco. I'm going to eat me some beans, then come up to the stage and kick your booty boy. Do you understand that? I mean, I'm going to take a piece of cow manure and shine it in your face, from the sun, because it will gleam in the sun. And then it will blind you, and you will say, I'm sorry. I'm glad I wasn't messing with Texas, because Texas kicked my ass," he threatened.

Then the singer said, "go suck a lollipop on a runaway train, you bitch. You couldn't handle the truth if it bit you on the ass! Get the hell out of here and leave us alone!"

I had no way of knowing that this was all part of the act. I was like everyone else and thought it was ad lib but when I talked to the rapper after the show, he told me the truth. I tried to tell him that it wasn't very entertaining, and he got very indignant and told me I didn't know anything about singing. He stormed out of the venue with determination to never come back.

I hollered at him and calmed him down and gave him his pay, but he left in a huff. My first encounter with the Chinese rapper was strange to say the least but I was intrigued by his music. I went home pondering the strange encounter and shook my head in disbelief.

I did some research on the Chinese Rapper and found out he got his start in Shanghai as a member of a boy band called Pay Cop. They did all these strange dance moves and complained about the communist establishment and the corruption of the bribe-taking officials in the government. He dressed like Boy George with an oriental flare. He had dragons on the back of his bright purple cloak and black chicken feathers glued to the shoulders of his outfit. The golden chestplate he wore accentuated the purple cloak and turned the heads of the half-drunken patrons frequenting the Shanghai Sushi Lounge.

CHAPTER 2

The next weekend I saw that he was scheduled for Friday and Saturday night and was a little dismayed. I had to admit though that his next song blew me away. It was a sad song about his mama in China and it gave a certain amount of acknowledgment to the beginnings of his rap career and the reasons he came to America in the first place. He wore his purple cape, and he had many diamond rings on, which eluded to his successes in his homeland. I was skeptical initially when he first took the stage, but his song touched a nerve somehow,don't ask me how though. He was sporting a scowl that let me know he didn't appreciate my critique of his bizarre act the last time I had seen him, but it disappeared when he started singing.

Rescue mama

"Mama, I love you, but your teeth are green.
You're the skinniest woman I've ever seen.
I'm going to America to be a rap star.
I'll come back and get you wherever you are.
Oh! You know I will mama.
My mama plucked chickens all day long.
She knew when I was born there was something wrong.
I was destined to be a thug on the street.
But the only people I could harass was poor people trying to eat.
I said, give me all your fish heads or you will die.
Mama wouldn't eat them because I didn't even try.
To get a real job plucking chickens to fry.
Mama, I love you, but your teeth or green.

You're the skinniest woman I've ever seen.
I'm going to America to be a rap star.
I'll come back and get you wherever you are.
You know I will mama.
I guess the rich people don't like the brains of a fish.
Every meal I ever came to had them on the dish.
Mama, why'd you work so hard to raise a boy like me?
Destined to be a famous rapper across the sea.
When I get rich, I will send for you.
I have to go to Texas and bash boy George until I'm blue.
Oh! You know I will mama.
His family gave me material for the rest of my life.
But mama, I'm having a hard time finding a wife.
None of the girls here like fish heads and rice.
They laugh at my rap, but they want a slice.
Of all the gold jewelry and the money pouring in.
When I realized it, I got wasted on juice and gin.
Mama, I love you, but your teeth are green.
You're the skinniest woman I've ever seen.
I'm going to America to be a rap star.
I'll come back and get you wherever you are.
I was finally able to afford to buy her the ritzy stuff.
Then I kicked back and lit me some chronic to puff.
I was thinking about her pushing the oxen cart.
Working hard to give me a chance at a fresh start.
I was rapping like a madman on a Chinese farm.
But the peasants hated my guts and tried to cause me harm.
I don't know why. My rhymes were very good, you know they were
mama.
Oh! So, I sent for my mama, but she never did show.
She was still stuck on the chicken farm so away I go.
Back to the motherland to find my mommy.
America said, get the hell out of here, you, rapping little commie.
When I reached Shanghai, I busted a rhyme.
Got the street vendors to wave their arms to keep time.
But the Army showed up with a giant, tear gas bomb.

When they found out who I was, they blew away my mom.
If she had only known that I could end up in prison.
She wouldn't have let me get the rap movement risen.
Now that it's here, I got released and I'm a star.
So, thank you mama, when you're jamming wherever you are.
She started to raise me right, but she messed up.
I became a star and she got killed. I don't know what happened.
They blew her shit away with a double barrel shotgun.
The only thing that was left was her teeth.
And they were green, and she was mean.
So, I buried them as close as I could to the scene.
So, I'm always sad because my mama got blown away in her hometown.
Now when I think of her, I always wear a frown.
Mama, I love you, but your teeth are green.
You're the skinniest woman I've ever seen.
I'm going to America to be a rap star.
I'll come back and get you wherever you are.
You know I will mama," he sang blowing away the crowd.

That silly, little dude redeemed himself with me and the crowd. They erupted in applause and gave him a good, old, southern hospitality welcome. Many stormed the stage wanting his autograph and the warm hearted gesture made him happy. I have to admit I didn't think he'd last another set before these cowboys down here would start chucking bottles at the stage like they sometimes did to shitty acts. Speaking of which, I guess his partner, the cowboy, sat this one out. I guess I convinced him that a makeshift argument with the crowd might not be the best course of action.

Before his next set he came over and ordered a pop saying he never drank on the job. He explained how he was a recovering alcoholic and drug addict after many years of hanging around in the opium dens of Hong Kong. He had a Chinese accent, but his English was good. He articulated himself very well and I was surprised at his intellect. He kidded around with some of the other patrons at the bar and I have to say he made friends quickly. His band called him back to the stage as they prepared for their next song. The crowd was still somewhat reeling from his last song which gave a somber but enjoyable mood to the atmosphere. People were actually anxious to hear what else he had to say. I sold many drinks and got some major tips as people were complimenting the new attraction, to our off the beaten path lounge.

"I thought this Shanghai Sushi Lounge was just your run of the mill dump but that guy's pretty good," one customer said.

"Yeah man, why didn't you tell us about this here Chinese rapper? He's actually talented. Where did you find this rapper?" another one asked.

"You'll have to see my boss about that. I have no idea where he was found or how he ended up here but by the looks of things I kind of like him also," I said as I was counting money and mixing drinks like a madman.

"Hurry up man, he's about to sing another song. I have to see this. He's incredible."

I was shocked at the response but seen it as a blessing by the looks of my sales so far. I was just hoping his rude friend didn't show up, and I was looking through the crowd, for that cowboy idiot. Something told me I probably wouldn't be seeing the last of him. His band started playing another song as people were scrambling to hurry up and sit down to the slow, sad whining of a steel guitar.

I was still scanning the room for that nit wit loudmouth that turned out to be a friend of his if that's what he calls him. I couldn't believe that last go around when this goat roper got everybody all riled up, and I almost lost a couple of my favorite customers. That businessman had some deep pockets, and he was a regular here, and right about the time I thought he wasn't going to show up he came walking up to the bar to order a few drinks.

"You haven't seen that cowboy son of a bitch, have you? That dude was getting on every one of my nerves last weekend. I thought I was going to have to punch his lights out man. What gets into people like that?"

"I know, man, that guy was flirting with an ass kicking from the bouncer over there.," I said pointing to the gorilla hanging out in the lobby where he had a view of us out of the corner of his eye.

I kind of nodded at him as I handed the businessman his drink. I was putting his money in the register and pocketing his healthy tip as the place got quieter in preparation for the next number. I was thinking about the Chinese Rapper and wondering if he was for real or not. I was wondering what kind of strange life he must've had so far ending up a Chinese rapper at the Shanghai Sushi Lounge of all places. Strange days indeed.

That's about the time the strangest song I ever heard before was blasted across the place. The sad start told of another blues/rap mix that was sure to either please the crowd or stink to high heaven. It was dreamy and lofty as the melody drifted slowly across the room. It was an enchanting and somewhat mystical piece. You could make out the Chinese influence, but it was catchy, and I seen many people, mostly women being captivated and taken away as they swayed and quieted down for the mellow music nobody ever heard anything like before. That Chinese rapper was different.

"Dreaming of China, is the name of my next song and I hope you enjoy it very much," he exclaimed.

"Oh! I miss China. I miss my home country. Me so sad, oh. You know I miss that place.

I always dream of red commie China.
Hong Kong, capital of the long dong, song.
Shanghai, eyesore like a stye in your eye.
Shangri-La, home of the sewer water spa.
Beijing, the place where I learned to sing.
Tiananmen Square, I almost shot my friend Pierre.
Hanoi, where I learned to fight as a boy.
Saigon, where I learned to cook fish Wonton.
Singapore, where I learned to throw knives at a door.
And Bangladesh, where I got tangled up in a barbed wire mesh.
Oh! That place is kind of rough boy.

Angola, where I learned to apply rock 'n roll-a.
Burma, they found a trace of a heart murmur.
Mongolia, their food shot straight out my ass hole-e-a.
Oh! It was bad boy.
The Great China Wall, I wish my mommy would call.
Taiwan, their opium I got high on.
Tokyo, the butt of my favorite joke-io.
So now you know why I'm so sad.
I miss the place that me and my mama had.
We plucked chickens all day long in the sun.
And chasing rats sure was fun.
I miss all the children eating worms.
A protein diet to fight off cancer causing germs.
Over there they get fried fish heads and rice for lunch.
That's where I got my favorite hunch.
To go sing rap in a foreign land.
Everybody says, who's that Chinese man?
He's the best damn rapper you'll ever see.
Just listen and I know you'll fall in love with me.
I know the music's sad, but it will save your life.
It will get you out of the house and away from your wife.
Her griping all day makes you want to go away.
Makes you want to go lay in a pile of hay.
But I think of my mommy and I start to cry.
Somebody said, hey man, dry your eye.
Don't be such a baby, your mama's mean.
Don't cry, her teeth are green," he sang sadly.

Bad thing was it made everyone sad and created a somber mood that wasn't suited for consuming mass quantities of alcohol. He came over for another soda and I felt the need to ask him to charge things up a bit if he could.

"What's the matter man, American boy don't like my style?" he asked.

"It's not that. Your song was pretty good, but we need to shake things up and get people laughing. I saw several women almost start crying and it's kind of bad for sales, if you know what

I mean," I said.

"Oh, American boy wants me to rock this place huh? I've been rocking joints like this my whole life. I was born to boogie, you, American little punk."

"Don't take it out of context man. I was just giving you some friendly advice."

"If I wanted any shit out of you, I'd lop off the top of your head and scoop it out with a spoon. I'll rock this place or my name's not the Chinese Rapper, you, American little punk!"

"I'm sorry I even said anything. You're a little testy, aren't you?"

"I'll show you testy, my American brother, get ready to sell so many drinks your taps will run dry."

"Whatever's clever, little dude. Just try to lighten the mood a little bit, man!"

CHAPTER 3

"Hey everybody, the bartender over there seems to think I'm a little too mellow. I saw Elvis when I was a young man in China, and I know what rock-n-roll is about. Get ready to be blown out of your socks," he said into the mic which made people perk up in their chairs a little bit.

Sure enough, this dude rose to the challenge as his band started in with some crazy rock-n-roll tune that got people moving and waving their hands in approval of the uplifting music. I guess Xiung Xiu is his strange idea of Kung Fu or something.

"This next number is called, I Xiung Xiu Your Face.
Guess who's in the house? Chinese rapper.
Not that Hong Kong phony climbing up the charts.
He tried to take me out of the streets I own.
I showed him xiung xiu and broke every skinny bone.
He should have had more fisheyes to grow up strong like me.
I'm the baddest mamma jamma that you'll ever see.
I go up to the meanest man on the toughest street.
Show him xiung xiu before he even starts to speak.
He starts crying for his mama, I laugh in his face.
Then I tell them, you all, I'm taking over this place.
Give me all your money, jewelry, and everything else.
Or you'll say his xiung xiu was the worst thing I ever felt.
I xiung xiu your face to make you leave this place.
I xiung xiu your face to make you leave this place.
I mean it boy, it's not just the squid juice that I drink.

That makes people say, him taking over surely stinks.
I used to have my freedom and a little change.
Now all I have is a skinny mutt covered with mange.
When Chinese rapper took over, he kidnapped all the dogs.
Served them up at his restaurant covered with guts from frogs.
I xiung xiu your face to make you leave this place.
I xiung xiu your face to make you leave this place.
Sorry you have to eat this stinky crap all day.
Maybe the next time I demand it you'll go ahead and pay.
You punks think I'm fooling but after World War III.
We take over this place you got from your family.
You'll say, Chinese rapper predicted this, he was the first.
Let's make him the king so this crap doesn't get any worse.
Do you know what I'm saying? Texas.
You've got to know what I'm saying.
I'm the Chinese rapper, I come straight from China.
I'll come to your town and kick your greasy behind-uh.
You'll be sorry you messed with me. I'll show you xiung xiu.
I'll use it on you too, make your face blue.
Your mommy starts to call, she's coming down the hall.
Then you say, man, why'd you kick me in the balls.
I said, man, my name is China boy.
When my fans see me coming, they're overcome with joy.
Escalating your happiness to a maximum level.
It's fun to party like a hyperactive devil.
Don't mess with me, I'm from Texas.
I'll stick a bamboo rod in your solar plexus.
I don't know how to sing.
But I come from the dynasty of Ming.
I'm the best rapper from the south side of China.
I set up shop in Texas with a seaside diner.
I come from Chinatown.
People from that city all wear a frown.
I don't know why they don't like my Chinese rap.
I don't know why they say it sounds like crap.
It sounds good to me and as you can see.

I'm the baddest mamma jamma there could ever be.
I don't know what to do, you're a fool.
You won't buy my CD, women drool.
When they see me coming, they always sing!
Chinese Rapper's the best- let's make him the king.
It's the best damn rap from the dynasty of Ming.
I xiung xiu your face to make you leave this place.
I xiung xiu oyur face to make you leave this place," he sang with much more energy than I've seen in a while.

That crazy little dude actually brought the house down with that crazy number. People were cheering like crazy and screaming for an encore. I can't believe this guy. One minute he's crying for his mama and the next he's rocking the house down.

"You, Chinese little weasel, who do you think you're trying to fool? Nobody wants to hear that Chinese garbage, go back to your homeland with that garbage!" I heard some heckler shouting.

I looked over and seen that stupid cowboy again. Oh brother, not this loser again, I told myself as I was rolling my eyes.

"Who said that?" asked the Chinese Rapper as he was peering through the smoke looking for the source of his loudmouth, paid critic.

"I did you, mongrel hoard piece of crap! We heard you can sing but what about dancing. All I can see is you up there trying to look cool as you bellow out your stupid ballads," said the cowboy critic.

"Listen here, you, goat roping twerp, I can dance better than you ever thought. I know you can do the two step and the rawhide slide, but can you do this?"   At which point he launched into a moonwalk and slid into the Elmer Fudd shuffle followed up by a sliding, air guitar move that impressed the crowd. He was running around in circles on the floor as his lead guitarist was doing a kick ass solo. Everybody was cheering except the cowboy who stood there with his arms folded like a jealous idiot.

"How do you like me now fool?" he asked after he stood back up and grabbed the mic.

"I don't like it one little bit. Maybe you should learn some new moves like this," the cowboy said as he started doing some lame dance.

People started booing as he was trying to show off completely humiliating himself. I can't believe this joker was trying to steal the spotlight from the Chinese Rapper. It didn't help his cause any because the crowd turned on him fairly quickly.

"Get the hell out of here with that lame crap. These people want to see some real talent, not some shmo trying to be cool. My next number will show you all what I'm all about. Don't mind the idiot in the back trying to steal my limelight," said the oriental musician as the guy was still doing his dance.

I looked over and seen the cowboy continue his weird cowboy style jig. He had his hands in his pockets as he was kicking his boots up in front of him like he was trying to shoo some cows into the corral or something. He became indignant as the crowd saw what he did, and they started laughing uncontrollably causing him to raise his fist at the Chinese entertainer. He was trying to yell something at him, but nobody could hear what he was saying over the uproarious laughter of the crowd.

"What was that you say funnyman?" asked the man on the mic which made everyone laugh even harder.

He finally went out the door in complete humiliation as the music began to play for the next number. I had no idea what kind of song it would be, but I was sure at this point it would be entertaining. I was slowly becoming a fan of this strange, little dude singing his heart out and laying it on the line for the crowd. By the looks of things, the audience was too as many of them were trying to hush the rest of the crowd that were still laughing about the stupid ass cowboy. It was more of a rap beat with clanging symbols, a horn section, and a twanging guitar. I almost caught myself grooving to the beat as I was mixing exotic drinks for the customers of this makeshift concert. He seemed to play off the latest commotion and accusations of not being able to dance because he was dancing like crazy to the prelude to his song and driving the fans into a frenzy before he even started singing. It was pretty cool.

Moves You Cannot Do

"Say bada-boom bada-bing, of Chinese rap I'm the king.
Do you know what I'm saying?
Hong Kong chicken wong, eat some wonton soup while you listen
to this song.
Order now.
Say ming ding shama shoe shan shoo.
Chinese rapper will show you moves you cannot do.
Aahso!
Shanghai squid gut pie, you'll love this treat after you get high.
You, number one space cadet.
Alimololly cangluwa samoi, a stick and a dirt clod you will enjoy.
Throw it at your friends.
Calla glue calla glick, I'll swash you with a tree of a lumber stick.
It will hurt.
Schmee fee calla glue can glee, I hope you have money for my new
CD.
Best crap you've heard in your life.
Now it's time to get down, don't wear a frown.
The best rapper's going to make you feel like a clown.
You can't keep up with the Chinese trump.
I'll eat your dogs and cats you dumb American chump.
Try to eat it with chopsticks, you can't do it punk.
A fork and spoon's not available in China, just funk.
The food tastes worse than anything you know.
And I hate it when I'm forced to eat it slow.
The food tastes worse than a dead fried pup.
Like a whale barfed in your cup, eat it up.
You'll feel strong like me, your enemies will flee.
Then they come back, you say, oh gee.
What do I do? I got the Hong Kong flu.
I got it from a man in China eating fish gut stew.
I don't want to die, until I get to Shanghai.
If I don't make it, ship my body you foreign guy.

If you don't, I'll come back and shoot you in the eye.
Now don't say nothing, just listen to me hum.
They all said I couldn't do it, now who's dumb?
Thanks for making me a Texas star.
People in China like to listen to this rap wherever they are.
My name is Chink Flink Stink with a link to Pink Blink Dink.
Go to hell if you tell a smelly fellow that his belly is yellow.
Now here we go, glow pro, you're going too slow.
Keep up with Wonton John from the east of Saigon.
My squinted eye spied a fly guy who won't buy.
My long dong, gong song that went wrong in Hong Kong.
My script flipped and skipped, and you thought you got gypped.
You can't get your money back, Jack.
I'll smack a pack of dudes on crack with a brick in a sack.
Thank you fools from drool school.
I bet you thought you were cool.
Buying this Chinese rapper stuff is the best that you can do.
You know you have to because I said you do.
If you don't, I'll come to your place and kill you in the face.
Then you'll say, man, this dude's a disgrace.
I said, I'll kill your entire family, your mommy and your daddy.
They you'll say, man, I don't want to end up in a paddy.
Wagon full of punks, that are drunk.
I said, man, why don't you buy this funk?
It's the best crap you've ever heard in your life.
It comes from China and I made it with my wife.
You know I had to do it because we do it every day.
We love to work hard and then we play.
The best damn rap in the Rio Grande.
No! No! No! In your foreign land.
Don't go away, I want you to stay.
Listen to Chinese rapper unless you are gay.
You know what I'm saying, you, little punk.
Why don't you just go and get extremely drunk.
Then listen to this crap, it's the best in your life.
You don't even want to hear it with your wife.

You hear it with your mistress in the hotel room.
You'll still be humming my songs in your lonely tomb.
If I don't make it today, my wife will kill me and then she'll say.
He died with a proud look on his face.
All the evidence was destroyed, not even a trace.
I can't help it you're all stuck in the human zoo.
But I can show you moves that you cannot do."

At which point he laid into a smoking dance routine that removed all doubt that this performer was from one of the best dancers in the nation. He topped it off with the break dance from hell that would've made the best choreographers blush with shame that they didn't think of that.

"Holy shit, that dudes good!" I heard one drunks say over the crowd which fed the ego of this new aged rapper.

I don't know what they've been feeding this little fella back in China but whatever it was started manifesting itself in raw talent. He was spinning around and bobbing up and down and finished it off with a shuffle and a slide that would rival just about anybody. Everybody was excited and ordered many drinks to polish off the night with a lot of laughing and carrying on. I had to admit I was skeptical but this Chinese goofball surprised everybody there that night. My boss, the owner of the place, even walked over and shook his hand as he gave him a huge envelope with a substantial bonus. He came up to the bar and showed it to me, $10,000. I asked him how much my cut was for getting everybody wasted enough to enjoy his show but he just smirked and walked out, cheapskate Chinese chiseler.

CHAPTER 4

People stayed late into the night after the Chinese rapper left. I made gobs of money that night and was more than pleased with his performance. I caught myself looking forward to his next show the next night but was wondering if this oriental dude could top his last gig. That dancing was enough to blow anyone away. I kept smiling to myself and busted out loud laughing a couple times thinking about this guy breakdancing like crazy. I was even humming his silly tunes and singing in the shower trying to match some of the lyrics I could remember.

Saturday night was a little more laid back than the previous night. I guess many people were worn out from seeing his show, but he showed up with the same amount of energy and rambunctiousness.

Welcome Wagon

"Now guess who's in the house? Chinese rapper!
Are you ready for the best rap you've ever heard in your life?
Oh! You, little American punk. You'll be sorry you messed with me.
A man from China.
Now guess who's in the house? Chinese rapper.
The Texas ladies say that I'm a dapper.
Don Juan living in a portable john.
I offer them fisheyes so that we can spawn.
They don't understand my China-Tex lingo.
But they always rub my butt for good luck at bingo.
How do you like that Texas? Woohoo!
I go to the farm and they start to drool.

When I fall off a bull into a pile of stool.
I rub cow dung in my eyebrows today.
So, I'll smell like Texas boys when I go out to play.
The best damn rap in the Rio Grande.
People coming across the border always clap their hands.
Saying, Chinese rapper is the welcome wagon.
Come on into America in the year of the dragon.
In Chinatown you stop for a while to eat some beans.
Made by cowboy Tex, the Tex-Mex, made to soil your jeans.
While you're standing there shoveling crap in your face.
You say, man, this guy's a stinking disgrace.
While you're holding your nose and ripping machine gun farts.
You'll say, man, Chinese rapper has perfected the art.
Of serving brains and fisheyes not so bad each day.
Texas is the place we want our family to stay.
How do you like that America?
Me from China.
Welcome to America, buy some rotten, jumping beans.
They make your guts explode like nitroglycerin.
Come try cowboy Tex's Chinese fisheye feast.
Listen to Chinese rapper, it's a very least.
That you can do to prove that you're a blind sheep, yellow belly turd.
And then you'll say, man, this Chinese rap is the best crap I've ever heard.
Do you know what I'm saying Texas? Are you with me?
All you, cowboys out there, rubbing cow manure in your eyebrows.
Oh! I hope you're with me. You come to my restaurant.
I'll see you there. You'll order egg drop soup.
I'll never tell you, it's not chicken eggs, it's ostrich eggs.
Oh! Now you know secret to recipe. Now, go to hell Texas."

I couldn't believe the audacity of this guy singing about Texas that way. And by the looks of the crowd, they weren't too thrilled either. They were still buying drinks though but some of them just ate sushi dinners and it looked like many of them lost their appetites as he was reflecting on some gross subjects during his song. These nuts might be harder to crack!

His next song gave some insight as to what the hell he was doing in Texas at this moment in time. I have to say though that many in the crowd were grumbling a little about his lyric choices in his last song. Don't get me wrong though, the music was good, but it just didn't blow me away like his last performance. I have to admit though it would take quite a bit to match what he did last night. As the people were settling into their chairs from getting up and getting drinks and going to the bathroom during this short intermission, he laid into this weird music like it was from the Doors or something. It reminded me of Riders on the Storm because it was interlaced with rolling thunder sounds adding to the mystique of the atmosphere at that moment which caught the attention of the crowd. They seemed to be captivated by it and I was also.

My New Texas Mommy

"I miss the smell of rotten fish in the air.
Cow manure and rotten chili just can't compare.
I wish I had some money to send for my mommy.
The government over here says I'm a yellow belly commie.
My new Texas mommy is fat and mean.
She has more warts on her lips than anyone I've seen.
Her donkey training gig never leaves her lonely.
The daddy of her garbage son was the only.
Cowboy who tackled that dirty, sleazy hide.
He fell off his bucking bronco, elephant ass bride.
The goofy rodeo clown was so drunk his face was red.
But he got back up and stumbled, and then she kicked him in the head.
He never got up again, because she got on top and kept bucking.
He was buried in the mud the next morning when she finally got up and started clucking.
She said, where did he go? My man must've gone insane.

Oh! Then she looked down and seen a hog eating part of his brain.
You come from a long line of cowboy clown queers.
Roll down your cowboy hat flap so you don't get a sunburn on your ears.
What do you use to make your mustache swirl?
How long has it been since you've seen a real girl?
That fart filled rubber doll has a pin hole in its mouth.
Will somebody please kick me in the ass forever coming down south?
Because the cowboy gave it a kiss with his cigarette lit.
When it blew up, I thought the Texas panhandle split.
His mama cut the cheese at that very same time.
Her Texas-sized machine-gun farts made her altitude climb.
Oh! She was very high in the air, man, I couldn't hardly see her no more.
When she finally started coming down to earth.
She screamed, 'watch out you cowboy idiot, or we'll have a backwards birth'.
The cowboy couldn't move, and he was looking straight up.
We pulled him out, but he lost his hat and coffee cup.
The truck we tried blew up that big, old, diesel motor.
But when the team of horses worked, we smelled the worst odor.
I said, man, you just had to kiss that fart-filled rubber doll, didn't you?
People heard the explosion on China's Great Wall, you fool.
I took my songs and left their stinky donkey farm.
Because the nasal trauma might do my rap voice harm.
That lard ass, ugly mama and her sewer smelling kid.
Gave me a lifetime of Chinese rap material, and that's exactly what I did."

People were laughing pretty hard during and after his song because he was making funny gestures symbolizing what he was singing about. It was entertaining, but I was beginning to wonder if he was a singer or a stand-up comedian. I was almost expecting that dumbass cowboy to show up and start heckling this guy again, but I looked around and didn't see hide or hair of the disgruntled ranch hand.

"That little dude's awfully funny! Where the hell did you find this guy?" one of the customers asked.

"I'm not quite sure. I think my boss found him in Chinatown over in Houston or something," I told him.

"Well, he's pretty good wherever they found him. I haven't seen my old lady laugh so hard for a while."

I was also wondering where they found this dude. He was remarkable in the sense of being like nothing I had ever seen before. There were a few cowboys in the crowd that didn't seem to appreciate his references to Texas. A few of them were getting mad, I could tell by their folded-up arms. Most however realized it was just this Chinese man complaining about his lot in life which a lot of us do from time to time. The Chinese Rapper seemed to sense this also and kind of capitalized off it, judging from the subject matter of the next song which didn't calm the seething disrespect brewing in the minds of some of his newly formed critics.

Jealousy

"Oh! Get down. You know I'm the coolest rapper you've ever seen.
I have a Honda moped that's painted green.
Why do you always laugh and call me a dumb ass?
I always pass you up when you stop for gas.
Ho! Ho! You see me on the highway when the traffic stops.
And get jealous when I use the shoulder to go around the cops.
My moped's there first when you show up to work.
I'm there talking to your boss about that stupid jerk.
That harassed Chinese rapper for trying to save fuel.
Ha! Ha! You have no job. Now who's cool?
You're digging in the gutter and picking up cans.
You say, I shouldn't have crossed the rapper from the foreign land.
Oh! Look at him sitting there with a pack of girls.

That little punk.
Rubbing his gold jewelry and running their fingers through his curls.
When you see your daughter sitting on his lap.
Oh! Sorry.
You blow your stack because you can't take any more of this crap.
Then you charge me but your daughter steps in between.
She said, daddy I'm leaving with him because he's the best I've seen.
Oh! You know I am.
We hopped on my moped and flipped you the bird.
I say, why is he so jealous? She said, your rap he's never heard.
He tried to mow us down, so I went to the marketplace.
He ran over 50 fruit carts, but he kept up the pace.
Then I took him to the beach to get lost in the crowd.
But he mowed over innocent people as he cried out loud.
The crowd chased him down and held him for police.
Oh! Then I did it with his daughter 100 times at least.
You know what we were doing boy.
You know I had to get down with that little lady.
You get a letter in jail with a picture of the kid.
But when she started to get jealous, of her I had to get rid.
So, you see another picture of me surrounded by baby dolls.
The one, of your daughter gets you bouncing off the walls.
She's halfway through a wood-chipper begging for her life.
Cramping my style with her bitching, I don't need a wife.
So, I heard you hung yourself and I'm very sorry.
I felt so bad I went out and bought a new black Ferrari.
Know what I'm saying?"

The place was silent for a while and I think I was standing there with my mouth agape. I looked around at the stunned patrons and then looked at the Chinese Rapper and his eyes got really big when he realized they weren't clapping. That's when all hell busted loose and many of the hardcore cowboys in the crowd started storming the stage as some of the others started booing. The wives seemed to be attempting to hold them back and the bouncers headed towards the stage to stop the mayhem. The Chinese rapper was ducking as beer bottles started flying and smashing on the wall behind him. Him and the band disappeared backstage as the bouncers were fighting the customers and not fairing too well. Wow, what a shitshow this turned out to be.

What a difference 24 hours makes. One night he was on top of the world and the newest rapper to join the music scene and the next thing you know he was almost tarred and feathered and ran out of town. The following Monday I came in and the janitors were still cleaning up the mess from the Saturday night riot. It was a slow week and it seemed like we lost several repeat customers. I saw the poster for the next Friday night show in the parking lot on the window of our establishment and somebody drew a mustache on the Chinese Rapper that made him look like Boris Smedly or something. It almost made him appear to be more sinister than he was already which only heightened his notoriety with the local drunks. I had no idea what to expect when his show started Friday night, but he showed up with bells on and started singing.

Party on the Farm

"Come to Texas to bebop until you drop.
You'll get the electric chair for a 187 on a cop.
We two-step to rap to start the party.
Then throw bull crap on anyone who's tardy.
Their boots jingle when they do the square dance.
Showed me lightning fast moves as if they had a chance.
To keep up with Chinese rapper, he was trained in Shanghai.
All the cowgirls say, hey, who's that foreign guy?
I come from a village 14,000 miles to the east.
Oh! I was chased by cowboys 100 times at least.
They were going to hang me, but I disappeared like a ninja.
Reappeared as the cook and added poison to injure.
All the cowboys that tried to kill Chinese rapper.
Most of them died with their heads in the crapper.
The cowgirls thought they died because they were drunk.

Then they went to Chinese rapper, showed him their junk in the trunk.
Oh! You know I liked it.
Texas Rangers showed up and tried to make me stop rapping.
But when the crowd heard my grooves, they all started clapping.
So, in the Lone Star state I thinned out the cowboys.
The rest of us got used like a bunch of boy toys.
Now you know why Texas is my favorite state.
They give you a hearty helping of fisheyes on your plate.
I took over the state, now I'm citizen number one.
Making you feel like a loser was a lot of fun.
Oh yeah! I have to go now because my mommy's calling.
Her favorite chicken died, and I started bawling.
I'll have to find a way to take the Orient express.
A cowboy sold me a ticket for 50 dollars more or less.
I got trapped in a boxcar in the summer sun.
If I get out of here, I'm going to kill someone.
I started to die of thirst, so I will sing this song.
Of how the cowboy tricked the rapper from West Hong Kong.
Squid gut pie will blind you if it gets in your eye.
Eating fisheyes will help you see again," he was singing but then was sidetracked by his dumb cowboy antagonist again.

"I'll Hong Kong phooey your face so bad you'll be sorry you were ever born. I'll show you some xiung xiu, you little pansies," he sang directed at the cowboy heckler I noticed at the back of the room.

"Who is this red commie, yellow wig wammee, piece of garbage trying to sing rap? It sounds like jap crap, that hit the trap. And if I see this boy I'll be beginning to slap. What is worse? This Texas, bean eating, little, chili eating, little puke? Or that Chinese piece of chili stain of a man? I don't know, he's an Oriental little weasel," the cowboy sang indignantly mocking the Chinese Rapper.

Oh brother, not this schtick again. I almost started laughing at the absurdity of the situation, but the crowd beat me to it. I looked up at the rapper and he was rolling his eyes and looking at the heckler like he didn't give a damn about his crybaby insult. I guess it was entertaining in a sick sort of way. I was thinking, 'what's the world coming to that this is considered to be American showmanship?' What a joke!

He strutted off the stage like a proud peacock high stepping through tall cotton flapping his arms. If he calls this a victory I'd hate to see what a loss would be. After he left for his break the cowboy came up and ordered a beer and informed me he was going to kill that guy one of these nights. I looked at him skeptically as I handed him his beer and he sneered at me for not believing his threat.

CHAPTER 5

After the cowboy finally sat down following many insults and laughs the Chinese Rapper continued his show. His next song was a dis track aimed at his number one nemesis.

Cowboy and His Mama

"Me Chinese rapper, I smell like fish.
Rotten beans and fish brains is my favorite dish.
I wrote the long dong, gong song that went wrong in Hong Kong.
The cowboy's mama does the two-step when she hears this song.
You know she does. She's a weird lady.
My name is Chink Flink Stink with a link to pink blink dink.
I can't tell between your mama and the donkey which has the worst stink.
I tell a smelly fellow that his belly is yellow.
Your mama's booty quake looks like a ton of Jell-O.
Oh! She's really sexy.
My script flipped and skipped, and you thought you got gypped.
Your mama turned into a hooker, but the gorilla squad got tipped.
You know they busted her.
Wong gong, chicken-dong. What happened to your mama made me write this song.
The clinic doctor looked under her dress and said there's something wrong.
I don't know what it was.
I hate to be ungrateful to these cowboy turds.
But the cowboy dissed my mama, so I wrote these words.
He said that she was ugly, and her teeth were green.

I said, I know you're telling the truth but you're being mean.
Just because your cowboy mama was the queen of cottage cheese.
Don't make fun of the lady that brought the rapper that's Chinese.
I know you chew tobacco, and you wear a cowboy hat.
You don't use deodorant and your mama is fat.
I know that for sure, buddy.
Your truck's a piece of junk and your tractor don't start.
Why don't you pound a watermelon up your mom's butt, so she won't fart?
You know she needs it.
She brings tears to my eyes from a mile away.
She made the donkey she was loving, run off and turn gay.
You know she did. It was nasty.
The cowboy ran away with the donkey to escape the fumes.
Then he said, hell no, when the hotel manager asked if they wanted separate rooms.
Since Texas made me famous, I sing the truth.
All about the donkey farms and the screwed-up youth.
They're always looking down their noses at the local Hispanics.
But when they smell your mama coming it creates a general panic.
If you were in China, I would swash you with a tree of a lumber stick.
It will humiliate the hell out of a hairy-handed horse-handler and a hometown hick."

Everybody was laughing and cheering except the cowboy heckler who was sitting by himself at the back of the room with his armed folded in defiance. He actually played it pretty good and to a T. He dared not crack a smile and his stone face was enough to crack concrete. That's when the rapper started diabolically laughing to the beat of the music. It sounded so weird but added insult to injury to the man who tried to cool the atmosphere but also whose callous reaction added a sense of hilarity I've never seen before or since. I guess he learned that trick in China or somewhere off the beaten path.

I looked around at the remaining audience and they were mostly all smiles and seemed to be thoroughly enjoying the show.

I was beginning to wonder if his song "The Truth" was actually the truth or not. Maybe this guy was the patsy for the Louisiana dyke explosion Spike Lee was looking for to complete his documentary on the subject. He sure looked capable of doing such a thing with his grizzled features and rawhide face. He appeared to have gone through some things.

"Where the hell did you say you came from? I can't remember what you told me the other night," I asked him when he came over for another soda.

"I never told you anything like that before, you, American little punk. Why so inquisitive to the origins of the best Chinese rapper you ever seen in your life?"

"I was just curious, gee whiz, mellow out man. You should be pissed off at that cowboy idiot that keeps messing up your act instead of taking it out on me," I told him.

"You mean my landlord back there? He's the man who puts up with my shenanigans out there on his farm," he said as he glanced back there and gave the guy a nod to which he nodded back and gently smiled.

He took his soda back up on stage and was getting ready for his next act, or song, or whatever it was he called it. I was beginning to think this was vaudeville or maybe I was on Candid Camera and the victim of an elaborate hoax. He set up a chair in front of the audience and the band started playing some somewhat sad music. Maybe it's another one about his mama!

Cowgirl Problems

"I'm the famous Chinese rapper from West Hong Kong.
I always sound better after you smoke opium through a bong.
I have to smoke all day before I bust a rhyme.
The stoners say I'm phenomenal once their brains become slime.
I start to meditate and float across the room.
Those hippies know if they crossed me, they would meet their doom.
I mind controlled my gang to meet me in the park.

Once I ditch the rednecks, we'll have a kegger in the dark.
If you party with me, you'll wake up in a ditch.
You can't remember what happened and your head has an itch.
You say, my head got shaved so I must've done something cool.
The mirror shows you're done up like an ugly, hooker, clown fool.
Beer drinking cures what ails your soul.
Me and my Chinese homies begin to roll.
My Datsun can go up on three wheels.
Our shotguns and automatics make you back up on your heels.
When you hear a four-cylinder whining and rice shooting out of
the pipe.
You'll know you'll get your ass kicked and your girl's drool you'll
have to wipe.
We'll have a party at your house with a bunch of bad ass fellas.
Then we'll leave you in a cloud of dust, bewildered and jealous.
Your ex-girlfriend says she feels sorry for you.
She's bringing down my party because she's feeling blue.
All her bawling made me break out my Bangkok stash.
Now she forgot she ever dated that broke piece of trash.
My lavish gifts made her realize she picked the right man.
Now she wants to tie the knot with the rapper from the foreign
land.
I can't do that, but you're my date when I come to where you are.
I have girls in every town because I'm an international superstar.
If you party with me, you'll wake up in a ditch.
You can't remember what happened and your head has an itch.
You say, my head got shaved so I must've done something cool.
The mirror shows you're done up like an ugly, hooker, clown fool.
So now you know my parties are the best on earth.
You haven't seen anyone so cool since the day of your birth.
You can't create such fun because you're a spineless wimp.
People that know who I am call me the psychedelic pimp.
When you see my whizbang low rider you'll let out a giggle.
We're on top of your ass so fast and my hair trigger finger begins
to wiggle.
I can't stop the hair trigger and it blows your head off clean.

The crowd on the way out said, that's the best party we've ever seen.
You ditch banging, head scratching, wannabe jester.
I'll crack your nuts with garlic on my boot to make them fester."

"How do you like my little friend there, the Chinese Rapper?" asked the cowboy when he came over for a beer.

"I haven't made up my mind yet. Some of his songs are a little unorthodox but he seems to have a pretty good band. What's your deal man? Do you really like this guy, or do you really want to choke the life out of him with your bare hands?" I asked kind of joking.

"He's alright when you get to know him. Don't let the gangster rap persona fool you. He's as gentle as a lamb."

"He doesn't sound very gentle. As a matter of fact, some of his lyrics are questionable at best. I'm beginning to wonder if he's playing with a full deck or not. What about you? Why the hell do you always get into it with him? Is this part of the schtick or what?"

He just smiled at me and headed back to his table at the dark corner in the back of the room as the next song was starting. This is getting weird. This Chinese rapper and Texas cowboy made a strange duo and I doubt they'll ever go anywhere beyond these lounge singer domains here in Austin. I was thinking about all the talent that originated in this area and was somewhat dismayed thinking this is the music of the future. Strange days indeed. Talking about strange I was wondering where this fool came from when his next song explained a little about how he ended up here.

Farm Hand

"I showed up in Texas, a washed up, Chinese turd.
The Cowboys love my rap, it's the best they've ever heard.
They showed me how to chew tobacco and eat beans all day.
Cut Texas size machine gun farts and feed cattle hay.
I met his big fat mama and smelled her armpit funk.

She was a donkey loving lard ass, but she had a lot of spunk.
I had to wear a gas mask when she'd breathe in my face.
With her rotten teeth and cottage cheese she'd get first place.
She beat her son with a chili-spoon when he talked back.
She pulled a potato gun full of rotten beans and pointed it at his sack.
The hair trigger went off, so he had beans lodged in his groin.
He told her to look, so she punched him where his balls and butt join.
He jumped 8 feet in the air and was running when he hit the ground.
His tennis shoes burning rubber and my laugh was the only sound.
She turned to me and said, China boy, put the leather on.
So, I tied it to the donkey and made tracks across the lawn.
I caught up to her son and he was balling like a wimp.
He said, he was a piece of Texas dirt and I was number one pimp.
To be like me you have to eat fisheyes and brains.
Then tie up your big fat mama with a bunch of log chains.
You pack her ears with grease and tape over her eyes.
Then stick a funnel in her mouth and laugh when she cries.
You put a meatgrinder over the funnel and fill it with chicken butts.
Use squid slime to make it go down and top it off with frog guts.
Pack snuff in her nose using a hammer and a punch.
When she has a fart attack and dies, you'll thank Chinese rapper for the hunch.
You, little punk, you really made me mad.
Don't make fun of my mama, I'll kill you just to make your mama sad.
She'll be crying all day about her only living son.
Poaching these fried eggs is disturbing but kind of fun.," he sang.

      At the end of his silly song, he was glaring at the cowboy in the back. He seems to be playing a dangerous game. Makes me wonder what kind of kompromat he had on this goat roper from hell. Maybe he owes him some bitcoin or something. I was serving drinks and trying to keep from laughing at the absurdity of the situation. He probably knows why this Chinese turd was kicked out of China to begin with. Many of my customers were inquiring about the motives of this oriental rapper from hell. I had no explanations, and they were disappointed. Much to my dismay but to the delight of the crowd the rapper announced he was going to do a duo of sorts with his cowboy nemesis.

Talk about strange bedfellows, these two clowns were meant for each other. They fed off each other's hatred for one another and turned it into a part of the act. I wasn't looking forward to this pie in the sky duet but was selling many drinks, so I was like 'whatever' as the music started. This time it was a country sound to the rhythm that didn't match his hardcore gangster persona. I didn't know what to expect when they started insulting the hell out of each other's mamas. Oh brother, another song about mamas, but the beat wasn't sad like the last time he carried on about her green teeth and skinny build. If she heard this, she would kill him for sure. What kind of person would make fun of his own mama? I guess the Chinese rapper had a rough childhood or something. The cowboy must've saved his life and provided him a place to live.

They got up there and started sparring and shadowboxing each other as the music was playing. They were doing some funny dances and taking turns like it was some kind of contest. Then they were exchanging insults where the audience couldn't quite hear what they were saying. They finally stepped up to the microphones and began trading insults.

Lone Star Roots

"There you go talking about my mama again, partner.
I don't know what it is, I left you alone boy.
I, I quit trying to, trying to make you mad, sonny boy.
I don't know why you got to do this to me.
My mama, she never did nothing to nobody.
She was on this earth before you were even born, you little weasel.

I don't know what it is, you're getting on my nerves, little boy," the cowboy said.

"Yeah! Who is this little punk making fun of my rap?
I'm a Chinese immigrant, don't do that, oh please, don't do that.
Do you know what I mean? I'll tell my mama on you," retorted the rapper.

"I was eating chili made out of Mexican jumping beans.
When someone brought a donkey, and it was sort of mean."

"Yeah! Yeah! He had to eat his dinner with chopsticks.
And the donkey was for his mama."

"She said, son, tie it to the barn and go get the cattle prod.
And then go fix some chili with some Cape Cod."

"Yeah! Yeah! That's where you get some chili, and you dry it out.
And you put in some rotten Mexican American jumping beans.
Then you put in some Cape Cod and you boil it.
And then when it looks up at you, it's very nice to eat with chopsticks."

"I blinded the donkey with a mirror so he would kick that China boy in the face.
But what it did was, it kicked his mama, and she went down."

"Don't do that to my mama.
Now let's talk about his Texas mama.
She acted like she was from the Bahamas.
She thought that she was very cool and very sweet.
But really, she had big, hairy warts all over her feet.
She thought that she was pretty like Cindy Crawford.
But really, I never seen anything like it, it was awful.
She had a big, old knot on her forehead that had mange.
And she talked this language, it was very strange.
I couldn't hardly understand because she was oh so ugly and mean.
That man, I almost soiled in my jeans.
Then she looked up at me and said, 'you China little boy.
Get over here and rub my butt, it will bring you joy.'
I thought that I was rubbing on some cottage cheese.

That's when she said, 'you found the right spot, please.
Get a firm grip and begin to squeeze.
Do it to me, don't be a Chinese tease.'
I thought a fat farm blew up in my face.
Oh! But it really was just his mama, covered in lace."
          "I went to China trying to please this boy.
I met his mama, and it didn't bring me joy.
Her face looked like a chicken farm.
Blew all up on her face and arms.
Her face looked like a squished-up frog.
And when she went, it looked like a cheese log.
I said man, something down there looks green.
Something isn't right and something's wrong.
I said, man, this lady, I think she has a dong."
          "You mean a dong-key, don't you Texas boy?"
          "You know what I mean, you little Chinese weasel."
          For some reason the crowd enjoyed this and cheered loudly
during this intermission to the song and then they continued. It
was kind of cool because as the Chinese Rapper continued his song
the cowboy stepped off to the side for a while dancing this strange
jig that I have to admit was funny as hell and went along with the
music.

          "The Lone Star State gave Chinese rapper his roots.
Down there. cowboys like, um, to lick the crap off his boots.
They know if they don't, I'll get out my Uzi.
Start shooting in all directions until my arm gets woozy.
We make them spit out their tobacco and wait for their food.
And ride around on little, mop handle horses until they say, 'that's
rude.'
Rotten beans are the best dish on their plate.
We torture their mama if they're the least bit late.
Oh! Sorry I did this to you.
They break rocks all day with a croquet mallet.
If they break the handle they have to get on a pallet.
A crane lifts them up to 2,000 feet.

Their final dinner's a small bowl of fisheyes to eat.
We swing the crane around until they're about to lose their grip.
Ha! Ha! The crowd will start laughing when their pants begin to rip.
That's the point most of them start calling for their own mommy.
In Texas, it's fun, being a rapper that's a commie.
Halfway down they remember about machine-gun farts.
They grunt as hard as they can, some shoot out body parts.
The beans kick in and the Texas sized farts break their fall.
Some get lucky and go like a helicopter over the wall.
One lady, when she hit the ground, flew up like a rocket.
Underneath her we lit a candle that I had in my pocket.
So, come to Texas and don't mind the weenie roasts.
Once you get in your ass belongs to the Chinese hosts.
The party you expected turned into a sour note.
When you look down on your plate and see rotten brains from a goat.
We'll make you write to family and friends and invite them down.
When they show up your dressed like an unhappy, psycho, killer clown.
They'll load them on a bus to tour where the rap star had risen.
Then they gasp in horror when they pull up to a Chinese prison.
There's a lot of tears and snot as they unload the bus.
Go stand in that line over there, and don't give me any fuss.
Thanks for buying my CD and funding the revolution.
All former CEOs have to lick up all the pollution.
Sorry I double-crossed you, you piece of garbage."

"Who is this slant eyed, little puke they call the Chinese rapper?" asked the cowboy.

"He's a patsy for the Louisiana dyke explosion," yelled someone in the audience which made everyone laugh.

The Chinese rapper seemed to relish in this comment and made the gesture to be quiet by putting his finger to his lips and making the shush motion and then he took a bow like he was proud of himself. The cowboy stood off to the side and folded his arms and looked jealous. This sure is some weird way to entertain people. Maybe these two do know something about that whole debacle. There were open questions about the source of that explosion the baffled authorities.

The show ended on a comedic note, but the seriousness of the subject matter overshadowed the brilliance of their performance. The Chinese rapper and his heckler were developing quite a following as word spread about the rapping and dancing phenomenon. People from all over Texas started showing up to these makeshift concerts. Minorities were intrigued by his, in your face style and the country fans came out of curiosity. The bad thing was the fights in the parking lot afterwards. My bosses were getting concerned and beefed-up security.

The rapper's entourage was growing, and he was attracting more unsavory types. He was relishing in his newly found fame and started wearing more gold chains and extravagant outfits. The next show on Saturday night was shaping up to be a doozy. The parking lot was full, with long lines waiting to get in and I was appreciating the liquor sales which were becoming epic. The partiers were spending lavishly as they wanted to be drunk and stoned as hell to witness the magic of this unlikely hero. The place was packed with crazies and they were eagerly anticipating the arrival of the Chinese Rapper. They went plum crazy when the announcer introduced him, and he came out swinging as he shadow-boxed to the music. Talk about whipping his fans into a drunken frenzy. Thanks to the security measures they were mostly peaceful, but they looked to me like they could turn on the violence if things got out of control. I was apprehensive about those prospects. This was definitely going to be a night to be remembered.

The place quited down when the rapper returned to the stage. Drunks quit hanging on each other and repeating themselves with long, boring stories and the girls quit yakking about the latest fashions and hairstyles. They moseyed on down to their seats to witness the newest sensation in nighttime notoriety. I was shocked to see the Chinese Rapper changed his outfit into a star-studded rhinsestone cowboy outfit complete with a ten gallon hat with neon lights around the brim. I rolled my eyes at his decision to sport some neon green cowboy boots and pants with dragins on the sides. If he wasn't such a star I'd think he was a clown in a Chinese circus.

CHAPTER 6

The band started with the oddest music that proved they were a force to be reckoned with and the dance moves the Chinese Rapper was demonstrating were out of this world. That little Chinese dude really could dance as he shuffled his feet with lightning fast moves and spun around like a balet dancer and grabbed the mic.

My Girl From China

"Oh! You think you're messing with a man from China.
I can't help it that my woman looks finer.
Than any hot mama that you've ever seen.
The only thing that's wrong is her teeth are green.
She makes me chop suey when I'm feeling blue.
And gets to my heart through my belly with her fish gut stew.
I don't know where she works, but she makes a lot of money.
When I show her my paycheck, she thinks something's funny.
My buddies say she's stripping at the baby doll club.
But she always says they're lying when she's soaking in the tub.
Her phone blows up, but she has a lot of brothers.
But with a family that large she'd need 15 mothers.
I have my cell phone, but nobody ever calls.
Waiting for Chinese chimes has me bouncing off the walls.
Oh! You know. If somebody don't call soon, I'm going to take a shower.
Then go out and blow up the damn cell phone tower.
Oh! Finally, the chimes ring and I do the happy dance.
But it was just the wrong number, so I pulled out my pants.
I lost it man.

I go hopping around the neighborhood sucking my thumb.
People say, who's the Chinese idiot, and why is he so dumb?
I saw my girlfriend and she say, she doesn't know me.
She started pointing and laughing and began to flee.
So, I pulled my pants up and busted a rhyme.
Everybody started booing, but some lady gave me a dime.
She said, call someone who cares, so I called my mommy.
I said, it's hard to fit in when you're a yellow belly commie.
She said, don't be a sick rebel, get a real job.
You little China punk, every time you rap you get chased by a mob.
But I said, mommy, I have to follow my calling.
To get my flows recognized without any stalling.
You know I had to.
Then I met David Koresh at Camp Davidian.
I said, I'm the new rapper from the other side of the prime meridian.
He said, you will be the cook and rap in your spare time.
While I was out getting fisheyes, they burned the camp because of a crime.
I don't know why.
Then I joined the group chasing the Hale-Bopp comet.
But they all died too soon, because my food made them vomit.
I tried to get the astronauts to wake up to my rap.
But NASA said, go on down the road with that Chinese crap.
I couldn't believe they said that.
So, I just started flowing, instead of doing it for a job.
I thought I was going to have to find a place to rob.
I got discovered on a Texas farm training a donkey.
I was glad to get out of Compton where they called me the yellow honky.
The cowboys hired me to rap for the ladies.
I played in the worst chicken ranches this side of Hades.
All the strippers and the cowgirls love to hear my stuff.
Then all the Bible thumping beauties began to take a puff.
The opium makes them all do the booty quake.
And when my raps are playing their bodies always start to shake.

It's a beautiful sight, so buy my rap.
Don't confuse Chinese Rapper with that phony Jap.
He always steals my lyrics because his envy is green.
I can't help it, I'm the baddest mamma jamma you have ever seen.
So, Texas, buy my rap, before I have to kill you.
I hope you ladies like it, and it's better than fish gut stew.
Come to my restaurant, I'll serve it up cheap.
It's laced with aphrodisiac and will help you fall asleep.
I'll take stray dogs and cover them with guts from frogs.
It loosens up your brain fluids and melts the clogs.
It tastes better than fisheyes, but it stares back at you.
You'll say, man, it's looking at me. What do I do?
You take the chopsticks, and you eat it. Don't you know?
Don't ever come to my restaurant if you don't have a lot of money,"
he sang but was cut off by the cowboy again.

'Don't go there, folks, the cheapest plate is 50 dollars," he interjected.

"It's got to be better than that American food. At least it doesn't blow out my booty. Oh!"

"Go to hell, you, Chinese piece of crap, before I come up there and knock your yellow teeth down your throat!"

"What? What? You trying to threaten a Chinese samurai? Oh! That's Japanese. I mean Chinese xiung xiu?"

"Aren't you talking about kung fu?" he asked as the band finally quit playing to listen to the argument.

"No! There really is xiung xiu. It's the favorite of everybody in China."

He started showing some xiung xiu moves like Bruce Lee which whipped the crowd into a frenzy. Many people joined the mosh pit where cowboys and rednecks were fighting with his bodyguards and other minorities in the audience. They finally turned on the overhead lights and security went down there from the stage and the outskirts and started pulling people apart. What a messed-up concert this was turning out to be. Many injured patrons were escorted outside with minor injuries as the rapper just stood there and watched. I looked over at his cowboy friend who was looking at me and grinning through the mayhem.

This had to be orchestrated somehow, but I doubt they planned it like this, or did they? What kind of bullshit rioters would come in here tripping off the hijinks of these two morons? I looked around the huge ballroom and seen utter chaos unfolding in real time. Some men were holding their faces and women were crying. Some others were laughing at the absurdity of these spoiled brats showing the world how good they could fight only to end up injured and escorted out the door. I heard there were more fights outside. The manager went up to talk to the rapper and he finally pleaded with the audience to stop the commotion.

"Folks please stop the fighting. If you want to hear some more of my kickass songs, you need to gather up yourselves and get back to your seats. Please calm down everybody!" he said.

"You started this anyway, you, Chinese little weasel, why, I ought to!" spoke up the paid heckler.

"You ought to what? You cowboy, hillbilly piece of shit! These are your redneck friends causing the commotion, not mine. My fans are the greatest fans that ever walked the earth and yours are a bunch of violent idiots. Call them off before I come down there and make you wear your ass as a cowboy hat," he replied.

"It's not my fault your rowdy friends showed up and caused this scene. I was just sitting back here minding my own bees wax as usual," he exclaimed.

The rapper was getting ready to continue his argument when the manager interfered and motioned for him to back off and sit down which he did. Things finally started calming down as the rapper and the cowboy were glaring at each other. If looks could kill they'd both be dead, but they kept their smartass comments to themselves to help security get the situation calmed down. Many people were escorted out the door much to their chagrin. Others started ordering more drinks and food and after about 5 minutes things were returning to normal, or as normal as it was ever going to get.

The band began playing again as the rapper sat there sulking for a few moments, but he finally got up and returned to the mic. After the tables were reorganized and the last remaining folks were seated the music got louder again and the lights were turned down to where they previously were. The Chinese Rapper started swaying back and forth to the music and was ready to start singing again. The next song seemed to almost explain his pendency for violence and his momentary lack of control, in the immediate past tense. The beat was catchy, and the famous rapper was back in rare form as he restarted his makeshift concert. I breathed a sigh of relief as his song started filling the atmosphere with a sense of normalcy again. What a debacle and testament to the lunacy of this strange character.

Prison Hope

"Oh! I'm tired of people laughing at my Chinese rap.
But when I put them in the spotlight, they shut their trap.
They think I'm wasting my time, chasing a silly dream.
But when they get caught up, they want to join my team.
We have them laughing, dancing up a storm.
It's better than Daytona Beach when it starts to get warm.
Since I became a hit, I saw America the great.
It's almost like being in China where in line you must wait.
I know they have more people, but the food is best.
When I ask for fisheyes here, they think I'm being a pest.
The girls behind the counters always laugh.
I told them to supersize it, but they only gave me half.
I started a fat farm serving fish heads and rice.
They all lost weight, but I had to do seven years twice.
The Fed's didn't like the barbed wire and machine gun posts.
They said they had a place where I could always host.
My Texas rap parties and my fisheye feast.
But the prisoners tried to kill me 100 times at least.
They heard my rap then shoved me down so hard it hurt.
Then they all started laughing when my blood began to squirt.
They all stood in line to each give me a punch.
I don't know why they didn't like what I ordered for lunch.
My Texas fisheye feast and rap party did fail.

I cried for my mama and began to wail.
But when they saw my show, they almost killed Chinese rapper.
They said, this is your last chance, now get your head out of the crapper.
When they really listened, they became a serious fan.
Of the dumb chink rapper from the foreign land.
I changed my name and became the prison hope.
By staying in touch with people who are high on dope.
They knew that with me they had a chance to keep it real.
I could make a lot of money for them to steal.
I became the biggest hit and the prisoners got rich.
Oh! The feds said, how'd that boy, do it? That some bitch.
Now you know why I'm free and I'm coming to your town.
When you see all my gold jewelry don't begin to frown.
That dumb chink rapper has more money than me.
But we made him who he is by buying his famous CD.
Do you know what I'm saying Texas?
I want to see all you Texas girls getting down.
You got to, you got to eat some of this Chinese food.
And then you do your two-step, getting down to this and don't be rude.
I know they love it in China and in the heart of Texas.
If not I'll blast them in the solar plexus.
I'm going to be the most famous rapper ever born.
I'll be in the movies and not your creepy porn.
Do you know what I'm saying? Oh! I love Texas.
So, everybody come on down and hear my famous Texas rap.
It's not jap-crap, it's famous rap.
If you don't agree that it's the best stuff you've ever heard.
Then I hope you die by tripping over a petrified cowboy turd."

"Go to hell, you little, Chinese weasel! You don't even know the meaning of work. The closest you ever came to work was when yelled at the dishwasher when he handed you a plate with a chunk of food on it," yelled the heckler obviously mad about the last line of his weird song.

"Maybe you need to shut your American face before you

say something you might regret," replied the rapper.

"I don't have to sit here listening to this Chinese garbage. I have work to do out on the farm."

"Go home then and bust your ass for your overgrown mama on the donkey farm!"

"Don't bring my mama into this conversation. Like I said before, she was on this earth before you were even born, you, street punk piece of crap," said the cowboy with his arms folded in the back of the room.

This is starting to get ridiculous. This whole schtick is wearing thin. I was serving drinks to all these people who thought this guy was the greatest thing since sliced bread. They were complimenting his dance moves and style as I was trying to figure out why they liked this garbage to begin with. About that time the rapper started another dis track aimed at his professional heckler in the back of the room, and by the look on his face he wasn't the least bit happy about it.

Pussyfooting

"He's been a pussyfooting around doing pussy work.
A pussyfooting around doing pussy work.
A pussyfooting around doing pussy work.
A pussyfooting around doing pussy work.
His name is the Cowboy and when he looks at me.
I say, man, he works hard for his family.
But really all he does is ride in his truck.
And mess around with people down on their luck.
He's been a pussyfooting around doing pussy work.
A pussyfooting around doing pussy work.
Do you know what I'm saying? He doesn't work.
He's just a pussy. Oh man! He really made me mad.
He messed with me now, I'm going to kill that punk.
I was going to rape his mama, but her breath stunk.
She said, why in the hell would you want to hurt me?
I said, your son's a phony double-crosser with a big, fat pussy.

He's been a pussyfooting around.
Do you know what I'm saying? Doing pussy work.
He's been a pussyfooting around.
You know what I'm saying? A doing pussy work.
I watched him one day, he goofed off like a chump.
Told everybody around that he busted his rump.
I told all my friends that he was a lazy geek.
Then I punched him in the face when he tried to speak.
Pussyfooting around doing pussy work.
A pussyfooting around doing pussy work.
That's what he does. He's a pussy.
I told him that his mama was disgusting and fat.
Uglier than a frog smashed on a railroad track.
He hopped on his dozer and tried to run me down.
I shot him in the head to make his mama frown.
How do you like that? You Texas, little weasel.
He's been a pussyfooting around. He's been doing pussy work.
He doesn't work. He just does pussy work.
You know what I'm saying?" he sang with all the showmanship he could muster.

This was actually pretty funny because whenever he sang the word 'pussyfooting' he would step off to the side and do this little river dance mocking the cowboy. It was funny as hell and hard to describe but the crowd loved it. They were cheering and laughing and pointing to the cowboy crying in his beer at the back of the room with a serious look on his face. He finally started laughing also and at the urging of the crowd he took a bow. Now this is getting strange.

The Chinese Rapper gestured for the cowboy to come up on stage and announced another duet. The drunken crowd was going crazy as he went up there and gave a symbolic hug to his unlikely nemesis turned ally. I don't know if this was supposed to promote world peace or what, but it seemed to be popular with the crowd. I didn't know what to think about this goofy ass concert. I was extremely happy about the boost to my liquor business though. I made a new drink called the Kamikaze Cow Patty which was basically a Mai Tai with a drop of chocolate laced with rum that would fizz up and melt into a cloudy clump. It looked kind of gross, like a turd floating in urine, but it sold good.

That's about the time they started this cosmic music that sounded like something you might hear in outer space or something. It had clashing symbols and a heavy bass, but the bass player was exceptional, and they even had a couple of backup singer women who gave it a Russian orchestra atmosphere. It didn't match the two singing but was kind of cool. As the music was playing the rapper and the cowboy were doing their respective jigs and dancing up a storm to the delight of their fans. They had a spaceship in the background on the jumbotron which matched the music and added to the entertainment value of this strange spectacle. I've never seen anything like it before or since and considered myself lucky to be a witness to this new-fangled sound that was cascading through the room like a waterfall at a toxic waste dump.

They would come up to each other like they were going to hug and then start sparring before backing up again to do their famous dance moves. The rapper was shuffling his feet fast as the cowboy was doing a redneck jig. I was thinking a lot of moonshiners would love this act but I looked around and these people didn't fit that mold. They were mostly tattooed idiots trying to be cool interspersed with cowboys and rednecks. It was like the cast of Easy Rider were having an aftermarket party or something. How I got tangled up with these late-night hooligans was beyond me but they finally started singing even though it was a strange duet rivaling Lady Ga Ga and Bradley Cooper.

CHAPTER 7

It's a good thing everyone was tanked up because this was turning out to be different, if that's what you call it. It started out good, but I was sober, so to me it was less than prime time.

Rhetorical Observations

"Bold hero of the sick, twisted nation.
You make me wish I had a ticket to the Mir space station," sang the cowboy pointing at the Chinaman.

"See everyone, a treasonous collaborator. He solves the world's problems while eating a French fried po-tater," sang the rapper.

"My noble lineage is not smeared by clown burgers. It's torn between the working man and hostile mergers."

"I know you're a crappy job commuter. And a superhighway polluter. I say, hey, ass fat junkie, are you going my way?"

"I don't give a damn about that booger cooking clown. Or you, blowing the butt trumpet blues all over town."

"I want to put a ruby on your forehead. Then take a slammer and a hammer and take it to your face.
That one has to do with the fat, lazy man. Piece of garbage."

"Get out of Texas, or I'll kill you. Me and Chinese rapper are going to kill you, you know we will".

"Oh! You shouldn't have messed with me, you cowboy little weasel. You, little punk, you really made me mad. Don't make fun of my mama."

"How come when she lifted her arm the BO knocked me

out? I wish your mama would pop those zits on her eyeballs. And get rid of all the moles on her lips. Do you know what I'm saying? You piece of cow shit."

"Your mama's so fat her lips look like a lip on top of a lip on top of a lip. I'm going to shuffle some rock cards on her fat forehead."

"There you go, talking about my mama again partner. I don't know what it is, I, I left you alone, sonny boy. I don't why you got to do this to me. My mama's been on this earth before you even born, you little weasel."

"I will Hong Kong phooey her face so bad she'll be sorry she was ever born. I sure told him. Didn't I? Didn't I? Yeah man, I got my burger. And it gave me power to be tough, thank God for that patriotic clown, Ronald. Then your big fat mama will start rustling cows and robbing liquor stores. She'll throw her Bible at you and hit you in the forehead. She'll bend over and rip those Texas style machine gun farts that blowout and damage all your nostril hairs. She'll tell her son, go get the donkey, don't be a little honky. I'm in the mood for love tonight; I don't want to watch you spank your monkey. She'll tell her son, don't go away; I want you to watch me today. It's a donkey life; this is how you pick a wife. Now, swat the donkey in the butt."

"Don't make fun of my mama you Chinese little punk. I'll come up there and shoot some tobacco in your squinted eyeballs."

"Yeah! I'll know it's you when I see a 10-gallon hat and a two-dollar pair of boots. And your six-shooting little piece of garbage hanging on your hip."

"Man, I'm going to take my 44 Magnum and shoot you right between the eyes. My mama's been on this earth since the day you were born. What's the problem? Don't diss my mama."

"Why don't you tie your mama up to that piece of crap farm truck? Hop in that air polluting clunker and take off man. You could feed her beans for rocket fuel and strap rollerblades to her feet. She can only run about 2 miles an hour, but you'll be going 500 miles an hour. She'll be ripping those machine gun farts and make that truck go fast as hell. Faster than it's ever been

before, you'll say, what the heck? I need to get this patented. If you ever run out of gas, just tell his mama to get back there and start pushing. Get a good grip for the machine gun farts. Put on some rollerblades and hit it.
Don't do that to his Texas mama, or I'll tell my mama on you."

"You mean that lady that first brought you into this world with them fish guts on her face? Fisheyes, brains, and everything else. She squirted squid juice in your bottle just so you'd stay alive. Man, I hate that lady.
She brought us the Chinese rapper, that sits on the crapper. I wish that I could turn him off by using the clapper. Funky rapper."

"It's like the oddest couple you've ever seen. Big, old, Texas cowboy with a little Chinese rapper. That don't make sense to me, what are they doing out there on the farm? Getting all happy, trying to please pappy.
You and your buddy are square; I wish I had you in my crosshairs. Now why don't you drop that mean mug and evil eye glare? I hate your guts, and you smell like a mutt. Why don't you just go and rub your mama's butt?
You said she was a cow, to me she looks like a sow."

"There you go talking about my mama again, what's up partner? I'm going to come up there and kick some booty in Texas boy."

"I'm going to tell my mama on you, and she will kick your ass. Yeah! I'll know it's you when I see a 10-gallon hat and a two-dollar pair of boots. And a six-shooting piece of garbage, with a red scarf wrapped around your neck. Driving a junkie, piece of crap, four-wheel-drive, farm truck. With that stupid donkey in a back, eating Mexican jumping beans. Feeding them to your mama, strapped on the back, with rollerblades on her feet. Ripping machine gun farts, making that truck go 500 miles an hour. Yeah! I'll know it's you boy, can't miss you, you little piece of Texas garbage."

"Okay! I quit it boy, I give up, you Chinese boy, you made fun of me so much you made me cry. I was going to shoot some beechnut in your eye, but you made me cry. Ugh! Well, what am I going to do now? I'm a cowboy with tears coming out of my face. What am I going to do? What am I going to do?"

"Feed your mama the rest of those jumping beans and get the hell out of here. Man, I'm tired of machine gun farts all-around Texas. With your truck flying around at 500 miles an hour. You ought to get pulled over by a state trooper or something. It would probably take a helicopter to catch up with that bean eating piece of crap. They should give your mama a ticket for polluting the atmosphere in Texas. So, go back to your horse stall cubicle and get to watching your corncob porn."

"Okay! Okay! But if you ever come back to Texas, I'm going to, I'm going to. If you ever mess with Texas, I'm going to, I'm going to. I don't know what I'm going to do. But boy, you sure got me. Didn't you? Sonny boy."

That's when some other heckler from the audience interjected and gave his two cents about the situation before security went down there and arrested the cowboy drunk interrupting the rapper and the paid heckler, or duet partner, or whatever the hell he was supposed to be. His drunken outburst was entertaining.

"Yeah! I sure did. Plus, your dinky little Chinese friend there. You need to take him back to Texas with you. Let him rap some more on that Chinese, fish eating, fisheyes, piece of garbage. I hate that rap, that isn't rap, that's more like crap, you piece of trash," this loudmouth hollered to the beat of the music making everybody laugh.

"Oh! No, you didn't. No, you didn't. Listen to this rap boy, I'm telling you. Listen to it with your friends. Oh! I hate you, you, American, little punk. You're going to pay for this, you're going to pay with your life if you ever come to China. You will be dead, now put your hands in the air. Wave them back and forth after you order some chop suey," the rapper sang obviously disgusted by the interruption.

A lot of the concertgoers were getting pissed off about the drunken heckler and more fights broke out spilling into the parking lot again. What a strange turn of events. Easy come easy go, I guess. One moment you're on top of the world and the next thing you know you're lying underneath it. That's what happens the moment you thing you have the world by the short and curlys. Things quieted down the next week and I was wondering if he would even show up after that last dismal performance. To my surprise he did without the cowboy heckler in tow. He would have to work hard to erase that stink bomb, but he showed up the next Friday night and somewhat rectified his reputation. The crowd was cheering and got excited as another unique rap beat started reverberating through the venue after the bar owner introduced the Chinese Rapper.

The Dead Gang

"You're sliding down a slippery street.
Trying as hard as you can to get on your feet.
As soon as you do, we start chasing you.
You better get away or your face will turn blue.
Run and hide as fast as you can, and you better not trip.
Because I have a machine gun with a laser on the tip.
Why do you run away, are you a coward?
Turn and face the man that stole your power.
When I make you eat lead and you're bleeding from your head.
Don't go to Chinatown to keep you from the dead.
They'll seek you out on Shanghai Boulevard.
The dead gang will make a sure your skin gets charred.
We got your number boy, and we know who you is.
You won't buy my CD because you spent it on the kids.
Oh! Those kids can eat dirt, now you got my songs.
You get Chop Suey in the box so you can't go wrong.
Put chicken strands in your mouth and start to laugh.
Jump up and down on the beaten path.
That leads straight to a party with some refried beans.
You get down and try to fit in but your face isn't clean.
You have Chinese dirt on your hands and head.
So, you have dust in your eyes when you get fed.

Cat meat, frog guts, fisheye's, and squid slime.
It gives you a gut ache so you can't commit crime.
You little weasel, how dare you gripe and moan.
This song will change your life so change your tone.
We'll tie you to a cable by your spiked hair roots.
Spin you around in circles until you give a hoot.
Hang you in the street above a bucket of fish.
Bounce you up and down and hear your final wish.
Then we'll lift you up with the crane to 1000 feet.
A crowd gathers below as you admit defeat.
People beg me for your life, I smile from ear to ear.
They didn't know a Chinese boy could create such fear.
I hit the release and winked and did the happy dance.
When you're falling to earth, you'll realize you had a chance.
To buy the best CD by Mr. Chink a.k.a. Dink.
You start to run in space when you begin to think.
Of the large, gasping crowd and the bucket of fish.
You'll be frantically grabbing for air but miss.
When you're crying for your mama and you hear me laugh.
You're overcome with horror times a million and a half.
While you're praying my crew strung up a circus net.
I caught and saved your ass on a sure-fire bet.
That when the crowd sees me break out into song.
They'll say he's the best rapper from West Hong Kong.
The ladies dance and cheer and shuffle their feet.
All the guys get so jealous they stay in their seat.
They go ballistic dancing to this retro stuff.
Then your body starts shaking when you take a puff.
The opium makes all the women do the booty quake.
They fall in love with Chinese rapper and give me all the money
they make.
You, phony piece of garbage," he sang with diligence and style.

I guess it was a good song and the crowd really liked it.
The memory of last week's performance seemed to fade away into
the history books of crappy duets like so many others. I bet the
cowboy is sitting home with his mommy crying on her shoulder.

His 5 minutes of fame came and went in the blink of an eye. I was impressed by his comeback but was wondering if it would last or not. This little dude was unpredictable and strange, but he did have good showmanship. His next song cranked up the excitment a notch with a louder and more determined beat.

Triad Collaborator

"Put your hands in the air and wave them back and forth.
Order some chop suey, and then meta-morph.
I'm the rapper from China, I have an ugly behind-a.
Don't you even say nothing, or you will have a vagina.
I will cut off your dinky, and then let a stinky.
And you'll say, he's better than a circus clown blinky.
I will eat some fisheyes, then you will start to cry.
And then you say, man, I wish my mama got so high.
That she never had me, and then I turned into a flea.
Started buzzing around your face until you said, oh gee.
What do I do? I got the Hong Kong flu.
I got it from a man in China eating fish gut stew.
Come to Texas!
I sing the raps that make the children cry.
I sing the raps that gets tobacco in your eye.
I sing the raps that make Chinese say.
I sing the raps that make the Chinese gay.
I sing the raps that make the others suck.
I sing the raps to make people pluck.
Hair all day off of their butts.
They keep waxing but it keeps coming back.
How do you like that? You hillbilly piece of crap," he said angering a member of the audience who was let down a little by his strange choice of lyrics.

"I don't like it boy, why don't you do what your Texas friend did, and get on your 10-gallon hat and two-dollar pair of boots. Jump in the back of that truck and feed his dumb mama jumping beans while you're going down the road, man, that would look really cute. Wouldn't it? A Chinese rapper in the back of a Texas piece of crap, junkie, four-wheel drive farm truck. Go back to Texas and China, you, pieces of garbage," the drunken loudmouth unpaid heckler retorted.

"I've got one more rap for you, you dumbass hillbilly, piece of crap," the rapper tried to say.

"Do I have to listen? Last time I had to stick ice picks in my ears, man. I never heard anything so rank, it sounded like some kind of a chicken fart, or something."

"Don't mess with me or we will beat Texas prisoners all-day long. They'll be sorry they ever messed with China. We will sick dogs on them and let them bark at their feet. You, American, little punk, me Chinese rapper, I'll kill your whole family. I'll karate chop your mama and your daddy too. You understand, you, American punk? Don't mess with me. I'll xiung xiu your face, I'll breath in your face and give you duck flu."

Good grief, this is getting sick. I can't believe I'm witnessing the rise and fall of a Chinese rapper that seems to be disintegrating right before my very eyes. He might have to call back his professional heckler because his latest one is ripping him a new one. I guess he should've stuck with the songs that propelled his career instead of introducing these high production stink bombs. He was hiring more and more dancers to back him up and singers also, but they weren't helping his cause one bit. One might even say they're harming him and giving him a false sense of security of sorts. He had about six backup singers and a dozen dancers up there shaking their money makers, but his songs were no longer packing a punch like they did in the beginning.

Talk about a one hit wonder, he wasn't even that. I can't think of one song that was worth more than six cents and a pocketful of pie. I guess his song 'Pussyfooting' was pretty funny and the sad song about his mama but other than those two the rest were mediocre at best and garbage at worst. Maybe I'm just being cynical, but people weren't flocking to his shows like they were, and my liquor sales and tips were drying up. So much for him being a master at his art. I guess his shortcomings make all the true rapper's talent shine even brighter. When you're bogged down with garbage and the anxiety of being a nobody in a world based on personalities you can get carried away thinking you can break the chains of obscurity and make a name for yourself in the field of your choosing. It became clear he should've stuck with plucking chickens with his skinny, green teeth mama back in China, if that's where he's from.

I was hoping for some better entertainment from this guy to increase liquor sales but as I scanned the audience, I could almost predict who was going to be the next heckler, paid or not. I saw this big, old cowboy with a giant black hat on and a huge, bull riding, belt buckle on with golden rings on his fingers and I made a mental note thinking he would be the loudmouth fool to ruin this next show. It's like a roller coaster from hell and I was catching myself wanting it to end because it was making me dizzy. The band, which was turning out to be the best part of his show, started in on another song that sounded pretty good and the crowd was responding favorably by clapping and cheering loudly. Right before he began to sing the music started mellowing out and getting somewhat sad and I was thinking it would be another song about his mama or something. A violin playing a whining melody descending form the heights of their incredible prelude of art was my first clue. His backup singers were humming to the music and his dancers broke into a honky-tonk type of number.

CHAPTER 8

Two-stepping Blues

"I'm so sad that I ball each day and night.
My life's a screwed-up joke and I got into a fight.
I tried to karate chop a man twice as big as me.
He spit tobacco in my eye where I couldn't see.
I'm a yellow-bellied coward because I ran away.
People started laughing saying, why don't you stay?
We need a rat fink in this Texas town.
The only excitement's when Fred dresses in a gown.
Sing more of your rap while we do the honky-tonk.
I'll get in my four-wheel drive and give the horn a honk.
Cowboys and cowgirls will come from all around.
They'll start to do the two-step when they hear your sound.
They danced so hard manure fell off their boots.
They started slipping and sliding when I rapped about my roots.
I don't know why they danced so fast to such a sad song.
I guess they were so excited about the rapper from West Hong
Kong.
When the song was over, they were still dancing fast.
Then I started laughing when they busted their ass.
It was funny watching them roll around in cow dung.
Then they tried to kill the rapper from the dynasty of Mung.
I got tarred and feathered and kicked out of town.
That's why this song's so sad and I'm feeling down.
It took a week to get the tar and feathers off me.
So, feel sorry for Chinese Rapper and buy his famous CD," he sang
elegantly.

Sure, as shit, that's when the man I spotted earlier stood up and started bellowing. Predictable old fart was hammering the rapper for his misguided takes on American life.

"That was a blast; I thought you were going to die tonight. But anyhow, this clown tried to sing that silly ass song. So, I told him, guess what? We don't like that in America. We have real rappers up here; we don't need that Chinese garbage. Take that back to your home country with all those fisheyes and fish guts and whatever else you have back there. You can throw in your CD player and play it for all you're dumb, punk friends back in China. I don't like that garbage," he said shocking the rapper from West Hong Kong.

"Uh! What are you talking about? That's the best stuff you ever heard. You, American punk, you, no good hillbilly piece of crap."

"I'm from Texas, the lone star state, and guess what? I already seen enough, and I don't want to see anymore. You're more like a lone yellow dwarf and not a bright, shining star. I don't want to hear anymore either. I already know you're the biggest piece of garbage on the planet," he said menacing the Chinaman.

"Oh! I'm going to tell my mama on you. If you ever come to China, I'll swash you with a tree of a lumber stick, you, bean eating piece of cow dung. How dare you interrupt the greatest rapper in the world."

"I bet her eyes squint every time she looks at your face, little boy, when you tell her about your lame rap career" he said in a condescending manner.

"How dare you, talk about my mama. She's a chicken plucking, badass worker from Shanghai, you overgrown redneck bastard!"

"Isn't she that lady with the fish guts all over her face? What did she feed you? Petrified ninja turds?"

I guess that really pissed him off, "Now you really did it, you, American little punk, you made me so mad, I'm coming down there and start putting a smackdown on your ugly face, you Texas little weasel," he said as he was coming offstage into the audience.

"And I'll deal with you later!" he said pointing to me when he noticed I was laughing my ass off. I didn't even realize I was laughing until he pointed it out to me. He went down there and proceeded to do some xiung xiu on the guys face and he landed a couple karate chops before the bouncers and security pulled them apart.

"Let me at him, let me at him," he was saying as they were holding him back.

They finally calmed down the situation and the Chinese Rapper returned to the stage and the band started playing again. Good Lord, this son of a bitch Chinaman is relentless and harsh. The next song had a honky-tonk beat but it soon became apparent he was mocking Texas and country music like some lame joke.

Two Texas Trolls

"Come to the Lone Star State, pick yourself a buck-toothed date.
She's been slinging horse manure all day and she won't be late.
Oh! Her deodorant ran out and the flies been buzzing.
Then she'll introduce you to her cross-eyed cousin.
You'll have beans to eat, she'll make you lick her feet.
Then her cousin breathes in your face and you'll say, for the love of Pete.
What was that? I, I don't know, it smelled like poop, I guess.
Oh! They do that two-step until they drop.
Keep going on the floor because they just can't stop.
You take a drink up at the bar and say, this date was a double-decker flop.
You pick them up off the floor, they two-step out the door.
Then you follow in your truck until you can't take it anymore.
Oh! You make the engine scream, fly past the corny team.
Throw gravel in their faces, and then you hope it was a bad dream.
But it wasn't, no.
A Texas Ranger begins to chase, it turns into a foot race.
Then you say, come on fat boy, keep up the pace.

You burn out of sight, laughing about last night.
Those two, ugly, Texas trolls made me see the light," he was singing.

"Don't ever eat any of this guys food man, this chicken plucking fool don't know how to cook!" the man said rudely after he stood up again and started bellyaching about the show and his restaurant.

"I make Won-ton, egg drop soup for your mouth to eat out of yesterday's garbage. So, I replaced the eggs with fisheyes, and replaced the soup with camel blood. Imported straight from Saudi Arabia. Argh!!!"

"That was the worst stuff I ever had in my life, sonny boy."

"What are you talking about? That's the best stuff you ever ate. It comes straight from China."

"Hell, I could've went all the way to Texas by now and got me some beans. You little, tutti-frutti with the combination booty, little punk. I need me some Mexican or some kind of America food or something instead of this Chinese garbage. I'm getting sick and tired of fisheyes, brains, and fish guts, and everything else."

"I will hurt you bad boy, I'll xiung xiu your face so bad you'll be sorry you were ever born, you, American punk!"

The ranch hand, or whoever he was, finally sat back down after many audience members yelled at him to. I almost started feeling sorry for this Chinese rapper son of a bitch. He had some talent but, somehow, he thought having these paid hecklers ruining his shows was a good idea. Some agent practicing voodoo commercialism probably convinced him this was a winning strategy. If he would just stick to the music, he would most likely succeed but these ridiculous shenanigans are making the audience mad and watering down whatever message he's trying to convey with meaningless arguments as he tries to hype up the hoopla. Might even be more lucrative if he would just stick to being a Chinese pimp and forget about this rap stuff.

I heard he had massage parlors from Shanghai to Bangkok and he was trying to sell them to a former president who always dreamed of becoming the biggest Chinese pimp in the world. He also had patents on body bags and coffins. What a sick puppy this dude is trying to corner the wet market on Chinese vice. He sure had an overinflated opinion of himself. This goofy ass thinking he could come down here to this famous music scene and shake things up, he must be delusional as hell. Nobody ever heard anything like it but that doesn't mean it's good. I personally don't care too much for his lyrics, but I dig his fancy dance moves and his band is phenomenal.

I was happy with the quantity of drinks I was selling though as many must've understood he sounds better when you're totally shitfaced. Some of his backup singers and dancers were pretty hot. He sure had a big enough crew of helpers and bodyguards also. One in particular was exceptionally frightening. He was a giant ninja looking Chinaman with a braided ponytail and tattoos all over him including his face. I was hoping I'd never have to tangle with that guy. He just stood on the corner of the stage glaring at everybody. When the redneck was giving the Chinese Rapper a raft of shit, he just kind of smiled at the guy like he knew he could kick his ass in less than a heartbeat.

I saw quite a few cowboys leaving but as they departed more unsavory individuals would show up taking their seats, so it was always packed. This rapper was becoming somewhat of a tourist attraction around here as I noticed people from all over the nation coming in this establishment for sushi and drinks and a rare glimpse of the newest rapper that was gracing us with his presence. He settled down from the last intended interruption and the band started in on some retro music with a heavy bass and a sliding guitar that went well together. He even added some pyrotechnics to the show.

It was turning into quite an extravaganza with flashing lights and laser beams shooting around the room. I have to admit if anything the guy was unpredictable. I was just wondering what the hell he would sing about next. Maybe his skinny mama with the green teeth or his new Texas mama he was so fond of out on the donkey farm with his paid heckler buddy. These are strange days indeed down here in Austin. I knew when he started singing it was a ballad about his love life and I was just thinking, oh brother, what now? Was it a sad dirge for an oriental stripper, a chicken plucking beauty from Taiwan, or maybe even some Kpop dancer he fell in love with or something?

Unlucky in Love

"Unlucky in love but lucky at rap.
I had to go to Texas to put it on the map.
Come down to Texas to see the Chinese rapper boy.
He will steal your women, but you'll still jump for joy.
Because you got so close to the king of Chinese freestyle.
I made her smile, we did it on the tile.
Now why don't you go home or walk a country mile.
Let me tell you about my girlfriend from Chinatown.
When she sees me coming, she puts on a fake frown.
I tell her I'm in love, she says, give me your money.
She said she needs a car, I say, yes honey.
Her big brother kicked my butt on her porch each day.
He says I get no sugar, but I still have to pay.
He stole all my clothes and kicked me out in the street.
All I had was my nut thong and the shoes on my feet.
Unlucky in love but lucky at rap.
I had to go to Texas to put it on the map.
I can't believe my Chinese girl turned me into a homeless hobo.
It took me a year to find a house and my life sank low.
To the deepest armpit of society.
I felt like a piece of dust on the ass of a flea.
So now you see how love has turned its back on me.
Turned me into a worthless slob that came down with a bad case of VD.
I thought America would be my Chinese dream.
Now I have to go back to motherland with sores that need cream.
Unlucky in love but lucky at rap.
I had to go to Texas to put it on the map.
Before I left the Texas boy said he had a place where I could stay.

It was on his mama's donkey farm and I could move in that day.
The Texan gave me a place to sing my famous gangster rap.
Down there the ladies love to dance to this crap.
When they're honky-tonking down and bouncing off the walls.
Their boyfriends get jealous and kick each other in the balls.
They can't understand how the cowgirls went for me.
But just look at my face and you'll begin to see.
Listen to my Chinese, country, honky-tonk rap.
You'll say, I have to find who baited this elaborate trap.
Unlucky in love but lucky at rap.
I had to go to Texas to put it on the map.
I had my suspicions about my rivals trying to stop my momentum.
They hurled insults through the air and damn well meant them.
They knew me and my band were just a little too macho.
They singled out my beef burrito and called it a nacho.
They fell for the drama but overlooked my broad shoulders.
They were suffering from hormone induced jugs and lopsided boulders.
So, two-step to my rap while I give your girl an order.
If she doesn't do what I say we'll kick her out at the border.
So, thanks for coming down to hear someone famous.
A lot of cripples showed up saying, why did you maim us?
Unlucky in love but lucky at rap.
I had to go to Texas to put it on the map," he sang gracefully.

He got a lot of cheers, but I noticed most of our regular customers weren't so convinced. Many of them were locals who appreciated worthwhile country music and this Chinese rap just wasn't doing it for them anymore. It seems the novelty is wearing off. Some of the hooligans loved it though but they weren't big spenders like the regulars. Most of the rogues opted for draft beer which wasn't helping my bottom line. I guess it was a good Friday night show though, but I wasn't looking forward to Saturday nights extravaganza. I showed up with a bad attitude brought about by this oriental jerk.

By the looks of the crowd in the parking lot this was going

to be quite a show. I didn't see his paid cowboy heckler anywhere but that didn't mean he wasn't going to suddenly appear like he usually does. A couple folks recognized me and gave me a toast with their cans of beer making me smile and it took the edge off my bad attitude. I guess these people were just trying to have some fun and raise a little hell in the process, so I gave them the benefit of the doubt. If they want to show up and buy a lot of draft beer and mixed drinks to witness this wishy-washy rapper with the fu man chu who was I to complain? I just hope they brought a lot of money to spend and were generous with their tips. When the Chinese Rapper performed well I sold more alcohol, so I was hoping he would put on a good act tonight even though I had my doubts.

CHAPTER 9

By the looks of things, he was expanding his operation. He had even more dancers, backup singers, roadies, and bodyguards. He came in there like the Dali Lama ordering people around and being obnoxious to his roadies who were giving him dirty looks as they prepared the stage. Customers started filing in at 7:30 ready to start rocking at 8:00. He took the stage as his band started in on some funky, rap beat Dr. Dre would've been proud of. Strange thing is as he introduced his song as Water Cannon his big screen showed images of people getting blasted by one as they were protesting in China or Hong Kong or somewhere. It was surreal as hell because his band members were playing the sounds of water splashing and you could almost feel the water yourself as these poor souls were getting blasted left and right. I noticed his main heckler was back unfortunately standing towards the back with his arms folded and a grim look on his mug, oh brother.

Water Cannon

"This one is dedicated to my new Texas mama.
Oh! Your mama will cry when she sees what I did to you.
I fed you french-fried frogs until your face turned blue.
Then we splashed you with panda diarrhea we got at the zoo.
Then over your head we poured chop suey mixed with glue.
When your mama showed up, she cried, boo-hoo-hoo.
We shot her with a potato gun full of dead rats and messed up her hairdo.
Oh! You Texas little weasel.
You got mad about your mama and tried to charge me.

But I pulled out a shotgun and blew out your knee.
Ha-ha! The old bag started screaming and she tried to flee.
We hit her with a water cannon, and I laughed with glee.
Ha-ha! Because she slipped and spun and ran into a tree.
The disturbed paramedic said it was a catastrophe.
I thought it was funny, ha-ha!
Then I heard you bawling because your mama broke every bone.
So, I made you sit on top of a beehive cone.
When you started running you passed through the water cannon zone.
Then the blast hit your ass and you let out a loud moan.
You were slipping and running backwards and sliding towards a pay phone.
I was laughing because the doctor said your wounds would have to be sewn.
Ha-ha! He was tore up from the floor up.
So, don't mess with me, I'm the psychedelic pimp.
Your mama was embarrassed and ashamed of raising a gimp.
She got on drugs and smoked that stuff they call hemp.
Being around you and your mama makes my style start to crimp.
Looking at your mama reminds me of a blimp.
And her cottage cheese and stretch marks makes my dong go limp.
Know what I'm saying? Know what I'm saying, Texas?
You have to know what I'm saying, right Texas?
I love you down there, love you down there.
I'm the best damn rapper from Tie Neman Square.
The lonesome little ladies love me at Lubbock's Lilac Lake.
My logic defies reason and my methods are fake.
Not buying my CD was a monumental mistake.
It's loaded with all the Chinese rap your ears can take.
Her phony hairdo was styled with a rake.
I told her to redo her rat's nest for goodness sake," he sang in the strangest portrayl I've ever seen.

   I looked back at the heckler as the music for the next song started playing and he was so mad steam was coming out of his ears. I thought it was funny and started laughing and didn't realize he could hear me.

"Kiss my ass, you bartender piece of shit," he yelled above the crowd.

"Go to hell, you, goofy ass goat roper!" I yelled back which got a few laughs

Yellow Hope

"I'm a Chinese superstar and your jealousy's green.
Your mama's the ugliest woman I've ever seen.
I'm a psychedelic pimp and you're a cowboy turd.
I'll have your mama killed, just say the word.
I'm a xiung xiu master, you're a redneck wimp.
Wait until I tell your mama she raised a gimp.
I'm the Oriental Mack daddy, you're a gay goat roper.
Your mama's an ugly prostitute that married a doper.
I'm the yellow hope, you have chickens in your house.
Tell your mama to tuck the cottage cheese back into her blouse.
I'm Won Ton John from the east of Saigon.
You and your mama's the ugliest people I've ever looked upon.
I'm a street gang leader, you're in the 4H club.
Your mama's so fat your car needs an extra hub.
Oh! I'm wearing sunglasses you can't buy, and you have a cowboy hat.
How'd your mama ever get so disgusting and fat?
I have gold jewelry, but you have manure on your face.
You'll need a crane and to take out a wall to get her out of that place.
I'm Chink Flink Stink with a link to Pink Blink Dink.
A story about you and your mama is called a beached whale and a rat fink.
I'm the baddest mamma jamma, you're a hick chewing skoal.
I thought I seen cottage cheese coming out of the window, but it was your mama's fat roll.
Your mama busted through the floor and made the foundation crack.

I'm a Chinese super fly, and your teeth are black.
I'm the yellow Shaft, your rodeo income's unstable.
They lifted your mama with a crane, but it broke the cable.
I'm the yellow Hong Kong Dolomite, you have the cows stump broke.
Unloading your mama with a dump truck made the engine smoke.
I'm the king of Chinatown, you drink cow belly wine.
To move your mama, you'll need a permit and a wide load sign.
You can't compare to me. I'll shoot your mama.
That big, old lard ass. You know I will.
Cottage cheese blubber will fly, it hits you in the eye.
You begin to cry, boo-hoo, and smell rotten cherry pie.
Go to hell you cowboy guy. Why can't you be like me?
Why can't you see? That I'm the baddest mamma jamma there could ever be.
I eat wonton soup. It makes me very high.
Then I say, man, I can't eat any more fisheyes.
My belly's full, I want to go to school.
But it's too late, I'm dumb and you treat me like a fool.
I guess I'm just a stupid, American chink.
But at least my breath doesn't stink.
So, go out with me, you will see.
I'll take you to the place that you want to be," he sang.

At which point the cowboy stormed the stage and got in one hell of a fight with the rapper's bodyguards. People in the audience joined him and it turned into a full-fledged riot. His huge Chinese henchman was waylaying the hell out of the cowboy as the Chinese Rapper was laughing and egging it on from the stage. Someone called the cops and they showed up in riot gear and started pepper spraying all the participants in the mosh pit. Some got in the rapper's eyes and he started bewailing and moaning his pathetic circumstance. What a complete shit show this turned out to be. I didn't know whether to laugh or cry, so I started laughing at the absurdity of the situation.

He sang some pretty good songs, but his violent nature and

thug mentality took over and he was banned from the restaurant for life. My bosses couldn't believe they almost destroyed the whole place in the mayhem that ensued during this ridiculous performance. I guess he turned out to be a punk after all. I heard he was singing in some chicken wire shit hole in southern Dallas and it wasn't going so well. A few months later I seen one of his bodyguards and he told me the rapper lost his gig in Dallas and I wasn't surprised. He wanted me to ask my bosses for another chance which I said I would but didn't for a while. I had enough of this oriental scoundrel for the time being. I never heard what happened to the cowboy and his mama once he got out of the hospital.

The only reason I documented the rise and fall of the Chinese Rapper was to show people the dangers of the thug mentality. If this goon could manage to screw up a promising career it could happen to anybody. This little dude had it all in the palm of his hands if he could've just focused on his music and stayed true to his art. I guess it's a lesson some of us need to learn because many of our most talented singers go through the same thing. I seen it many times over the years, but this dude got under my skin somehow. I caught myself actually rooting for him and hoping he would make it to the big show. I seen many acts come and go but this guy had something many people didn't but like a fool he let it all slip through his fingers.

I figured he went to China or Hong Kong or somewhere else in Asia singing his silly songs to someone who'll appreciate his style for a while. He might make it to the top once again in Hollywood, but I doubt it. With the vast amount of talent in this country you better keep your shit together as you make your bid to be one of the best rapper's in the country. After this debacle our restaurant and lounge stuck with more traditional acts, but I have to admit they're somewhat boring compared to the Chinese Rapper. Maybe it was the backup dancers and singers or the pyrotechnics he utilized but his act had a certain amount of pizzaz we don't see around here anymore. I was thinking, good luck, you

Chinese son of a bitch, wherever you are. Shoot for the stars and keep singing about your skinny mama and weird girlfriends. You might not have took over the Austin music scene but you certainly made an impression on me, whatever that's worth.

About six months later I was leaving the bar and the Chinese Rapper was waiting by my vehicle wanting me to ask my boss to give him another chance. He said he went on tour in Vietnam and made a lot of money but without his cowboy heckler his songs weren't as effective. We had a chat and I told him he didn't need some paid heckler to become a success, he just needed to sing some good songs and continue his crazy dances and high energy performances. After he assured me he wouldn't hire the cowboy heckler anymore I asked my boss to give this little dude another chance. I gave him a song I wrote for my garage band and he spiced it up a little to match his style and I had to admit it went over well. He opened up for one of the other acts and impressed his fans who showed up to cheer for the unlikely hero. The music he used sounded like a Russian opera that kept getting stronger with each line until the climax and then it waned down to nothing at the end.

Mashed Potatoes

"I punched the throttle towards thrill hill. I just dranks a beer, smoked a joint and swallowed a pill. A giant sack of potatoes was on my trucks floorboard. I was standing on the accelerator, I mean the damn thing was floored. All of sudden branches, telephone poles, and sky. Who the hell said that man couldn'd fly? Coming down first I saw the tops of telephone poles. Looks like the dumbass repairman hasn't met his goals. I broke off a couple branches on my truck's windshield. The trees told me my truck forgot to yeild. I finally hit the ground and my head got bashed. I looked around in my truck and all the potatoes were mashed. I started hooting and hollering but nobody was around. My truck steaming and a distant bullfrog was the only sound. The jump of the century and not one witness. When I tell this story they'll think I lack mental fitness. But as I picked up all my tools scattered about, I poked my chest out like a hero gladiator with clout. When I'm famous I'll remeber this story. The blood on my head made it twisted and gory. The dust in the air took a while to settle, took a while for the heat to dissipate through the metal. Standing with my hand on the hood to help it cool down, thinking of being a future superstar and thinking about town," he sang with all the showmanship he could muster.

The crowd was silent for a few moments but then they erupted uproariously. Seems the crowd loved the song and the video on the jumbotron of a pickup truck flying through the sky to match the song was the icing on the cake. The unorthodox Russian opera music gave a haunting aspect to the song and with that the Chinese Rapper redeemed himself. I gave him several other songs and wasn't quite sure which one he'd use next but I figured it out quickly when a video of him working in a dismal pit in some sweatshop appeared on the screen. It was a typical workingman blues kind of song and he added some violins during the sad parts in during the chorus but spiced it up with hard hitting rock-n-roll during the climax.

The Coworker's Curse

(Chorus) "I make minimum wage when I'm making your apparel. Stay busy or I'll kick in the gonads until you're definitely steril."

"Half of them don't even show up to work, and when they do they're wasted. How many different flavors of LSD this morning have you tasted? Your deer in the headlights babyface makes you look weak. Nobody understands the splitting syllables when you try to speak. I wish you could see yourself in that zit juice coated mirror. Wipe off the green specks so you can see a coward clearer. He's afraid of the bossman because he's mean and scary. He needs time off to wax his muff when his rearend gets hairy. He eats fifty pain pills when his wife pulls off the wax. His advanced job skills consist of scratching his gluteus max. (chorus) He thinks he's worth ten times more than what his paycheck says.

He can't stand my psychedelic robe or my bright green fez. I'm a super cosmic, hyperactive genius and he hates my guts. I told him his ass had more sores than hardcore, porn-queen sluts. He belittled my position at the edible underwear plant. He ate moth holes in the panties after I told him he can't. I yelled at him for munching down a majority of the profits. My castle has magic prisms hanging from the window soffits. They spell out disasters and warn me of any attempted intrusions. He's a meaningless worm inside a madman's menacing delusions. (chorus) He's mad because I control world events with my telepathic waves. I threw a curse on his carcass rivaling the scariest graves. He was a double-barrel dipshit on a double-dog dare. He threatened a pregnant mother of three for messing up his hair. He despised working stiffs and looked down on pedestrians. He went to the Kentucky Derby and insulted equestrians. I turned him into a sick bastard who commercially consumed himself. He got mad, threw a temper tantrum, and knocked his trophies off the shelf. If I can do that to a crybaby with a green bubble of snot. I can look at your pathetic life and make your bones start to rot. Your skin would dry up and your muscles will melt. You'll say that was the craziest curse my carcass ever felt. So stay busy at your task and don't question my authority, or I'll be forced to ruin your life with my mental superiority," sang the rapper.

CHAPTER 10

That song blew away the crowd also and the imagery on the big screen combined with his unique dancing set it off nicely. He thanked me when he left and my boss decided to give him another chance to headline a show. The next Friday night's gig was advertised widely and a huge crowd turned out. The Chinese Rapper thanked me again when he showed up and ordered his legendary grape soda and he went backstage to prepare for the show. I scanned the audience for his cowboy heckler and was happy not to see him anywhere. His fans were whipped up into a frenzy when he finally appeared and his band was playing some cool music. I knew which song he would sing by the bloody hands on the big screen.

Bloody Hands

"I heard you crying and begging for another five minutes. You're the laziest and dirtiest of my former tenants. Having the nerve and gall to request a refund of your security deposit. When every single problem we ever had you were there to cause it. Chucking eight balls of crack out your first story window. Giving all the female passerby's a sexual innuendo. Nobody wants to flop out their melons or sit on your face, and they don't need your various diseases in their nether region place. They'd be walking bowlegged for two years because of you, and the diaper rash on your lips made your gums turn blue. They reacted with your yellow teeth to give the aura of green. They would glow in the dark if a black light was shining on the scene. The pyorrhea pirate with the horrendous halitosis, that can't even be disinfected with distilled water or reverse osmosis. They can clean up sewer water but not your mouth. A northern windbag blowing hot air all across the south. Crybaby kindergarteners that fall for every fad. The most bandwagon riding marauders the world ever had. They jump on until the first sign of friction or heat. Then they jump backwards until the reach the former spot of their feet. Sticking their chests out and talking tough but getting nowhere. Then they resort to slinging mud and showing their underwear. Trying to secure votes from the hairy-palmed pervs. If they win the country will get much less than it deserves. We need practical world leaders not some nobody has-been, that has to keep going back to the drawing board of his original sin. Having to resort to treason, betrayal, and trickery. Bashing the brains out of baby seals with a hunk of hickory. Starving out little kids and forcing the elderly into homes, where thoughts of rotten sugarplums dance in their domes. They go hungry and die because of your conservative greed. And to create a price-hike of gasoline you send boys over to bleed," he sang forcefully.

Many of the onlookers were in shock by the end of the song, so I guess it was successful. They cheered wildly for the performer for the little dance number he did at the end which concluded in a shuffle and a slide. The next number had me guessing for a while because the jumbtron showed a filthy toilet in a nasty looking bathroom with a slutty looking rubber dolly sitting on the porcelain throne. A lot of people gasped since it was so disgusting but they liked the mesmerizing music leading up to the lyrics. About halfway through I recognized the song I gave him.

Joe the Plumber's Lover

"I'm falling apart at the seams because I quit having dreams. Everything's getting darker and I have no high beams. No secret switch to shed light on the forward path. My mind's a machine that mixes micrscopic molecules with math. They almost bent time once and ended up in a black hole. They said we'll be sucked into a vortex of the universe's lost soul. We'll be riding that runaway freight train to the end of the line. So give a toast to scientology with your finest wine. Impossible mission specialists will sort out the issues. If not you can buy yourself some of their patented monogrammed, baby wipe tissues. Crybabies, temper tantrums, and rich spoiled brats. They didn't get what they wanted and they had to eat rats. The masses shunned their overpriced Hollywood production, about Joe the plumber and his plunger with plenty of suction. He was a futuristic, high-tech, turd-busting spy. He tried to stay in touch with the youth through his mind's seeing eye. They saw right through his phony facade and shitty charade. It was the heftiest hunk of horse shit Hollywood ever made. They tried to manipulate commercialism to tell you what you want. They think your a programmed pea brain and a spineless runt. Trying to overshadow the younger folks with blockbuster actors. But they're just blue-balled bastards and beneficial benefactors. Always using golden showers to polish the corrosion. Every time their driver starts their car they wait for the explosion. They know a million psychos want to eat their brains. Zombies looking for five minutes of fame and finacial gains. Bag ladies and junk dealers can't wait to sort through your stuff. They'll mangle your man-made mistress with the mutilated muff. That rubber dolly you've been boning since you reached adolescence. Polly the urethane uterus emitting that malleable, plastic essence. You should call her Snowflake, the nympho dandruff queen. Bums at the dump will gang rape her until her skin turns green. Joe's beautiful bride will provide the local hobos with a moment of joy. As he's turd-busting Lucifer's sewage for the evil hoi polloi," sang the Chinese Rapper.

The crowd liked his rendition but I felt like he butchered one of my best songs. He added some oriental chimes and gongs that seemed to subtract from the potency of the original track. I always used guitars and deep bass rumblings but I guess his style was more fitting to his unique category. His next number seemed to denounce and condemn his rival in the Chinese rap scene overseas but was overshadowed by his special blend of harmony and rythm unrivaled in the American form of gangster rap. He had some bad looking dudes standing off to the side with their arms folded, I guess to intimidate his adversaries in case someone filmed the show and live-streamed it back in China. This impostor was doxed and called out into the streets of Hong Kong for a showdown at high noon and the crowd thought it was manly. This time he included some hard hitting rock music to authenticate his message to his fans back in the orient.

Kpop Don't Understand

"Kpop thinks they're the newest rage in Tokyo but turned their backs on me. I can't help it I'm the baddest mamma-jamma the world will ever see. He just keeps spitting bile out of his polluted gullet. He sees a button that says push but he finds a way to pull it. He took the low road to Shanghai and goes against the grain. He's a demonic simpleton who's obviously insane. He created a new brand of evil and wants it to spread. He looks like a Charlie Chan reject with a lopsided head. He was christened by the queen of Hong Kong and honored with a title. A crotch rubbing sissy and a middle-aged idol. He's above the notion that we're all created equal. His songs are like a bad after-school special or a low-budget sequel. He brought shame to eastern rap and destroyed its meaning. He's a spoiled brat silver spoon who still needs weaning. I guess by now you've noticed I hate his puke-filled guts. I have more respect for crackheads and crank-whore sluts. At least they're real and down to earth. He's been stinking up the airways since the day of my birth. He should've rode some other bandwagon of apocalyptic doom. Instead of burying oriental rap in a silly looking tomb. He deserves a death-blow delivered to his disgusting face. He needs to quit turning stomachs and wasting space. He wears windshield-wiper sunglasses to keep his sight clear. He sings songs about bravery while drowning in fear. He's a sanctimonious scoundrel with a swollen sphincter. He eclipsed a beautiful princess and somehow shrinked her. She sought shelter in the protective wings of his peaceful pod. He raped her respected reputation with a Roto-Rooter rod. Her causes seemed to fade away and paled in comparison. To him setting up his rap kingdom with a castle and garrison. Coasting through life with a chuckwagon of over-rated hits. He poisoned our youngster's minds and gave them the shits. They started betraying their friends and brutalizing their neighbors. Just because some imperialistic swine christened him with their magic sabers. I'm the only one willing and able to take you where you need to be. So make Chinese Rapper a superstar by buying his famous CD," he sang proudly and masterfully.

Talk about a strange turn of events but the crowd cheered wildly for the Chinese Rapper as he exited the stage. He ended the song with a lot of pyrotechnics and the smoke was still lingering in the air when the lights came on and fans started making their way to the exits. I heard some commotion up by the stage and realized he was up there signing new CDs for his loyal fans. It caused quite a ruckus as people leaving were bumping into others on their way back in once they heard what he was doing. I was very happy with the liquor sales and big tips from his upscale oriental fans. About an hour later as the crowd was thinning he approached my bar and asked me how I liked the show. I told him it was a good night and his music was lively and inspiring. He offered me an invitaion to his restaurant/opium den but I told him I didn't do that stuff so we made plans to meet at a barbeque place after the show before he returned backstage to get ready for his grand finale.

Shake It

"Shake it to the left, shake it to the right.
Shake it like a bowl of Jello with all your might.
You know shaking it drives everybody crazy.
Even spun-out junkies who are hungry and lazy.
They spent their food money on drugs and crumbs.
Nibbling on them later as they're begging from bums.
They walk up to winos demanding their goods.
Stealing pocket lent and empty bottles wearing long, black hoods.

I know that you know and you know that I know.
Maturity and muscles are things you never watch grow.
You're trapped in a viscious cycle spinning around.
Your thoughts and ideas aren't world renown.
You always get pissed off when you have to think.
Because you can't save the princess when you have to blink.
Superheroes were not meant to exert physical force.
They always have some magic power and secret source.
A hidden level a gladiator maestro could seldom reach.
You have electronic walls to smash and dykes to breach.
Hong Kong hackers will honor your fame.
Tokyo whiz kids will cherish your name.
Remote, third-world villagers will make a pilgramage to your house.
Even crazy Cambodians and the Khmer Rouge in Laos.
They want your ugly mug gracing their wall of death.
Since they know you cheated using steroids and meth.
Staying up all night banging on your controller.
The sugary foods you craved left a hole in your molar.
So do the shake, shake, jiggle dance as a preemptive maneuver.
Then you can hide out in a rickety shack in Northern Vancouver.
Let the storm clouds blow over, then you can blossom.
You can eat berries, roots, and barbequed possum.
You'll be high-stepping through tall cotton flapping your arms.
Living like a lackluster leprichan who loves his Lucky Charms.
Shake it like you mean it, you video game warrior.
If you get busted shaking your booty I'll loan you my checkered pants lawyer," he sang doing a dance like he was playing a video game shaking his money-maker.

It was kind of cool because the jumbotron had some bizarre video game I had never seen before and when the character ate a money chip he'd stop and shake his rear end like he was mocking the powers that be. Adding some muical notes that resembled the Mario Brother's game seemed to emphasize the absurdity he obviously felt was ingrained in the video game industry. The crowd seemed to enjoy his show and he went backstage only to be recalled for a encore performance and the crowd went wild when he reappeared doing his shuffle and slide routine showing off his unique dance skills. The band started in with some southern rockabilly music and visions of the swamp were projected on the big screen behind the Chinese rapper giving a strange, green glow to the room as the sounds of crickets and bullfrogs provided a musical backdrop to the fading in twanging intro as the steel guitar whined to the rythm of the swamp and I have to admit it seemed to mesmerize the audience.

Stuck in the Muck

"I'm singing about the mud at the bottom of the swamp, where the flatheads sleep and reptiles romp.
Oil kills or injures everything in sight, they said it was a mild form of poison but that's not right.
They had to minimize panic and control your psyche, if you don't like blackened shrimp hand them to Mikey.
That dumb, little batsard will eat just about anything, give him all the toxic waste the waitress can bring.
He's been eating commercialized garbage and he's fully immune, he has the gut of a gas guzzling goober and a gimp goosing goon.
He makes fun of women's faces like a carpel tunnel creep, his hairy palms and chrome dome disturbs them in their sleep.
The bald-headed werewolf from south Louisiana, stalking victims under the blood moon in a red bandana.
Everyone knows he's bald under that Aunt Jemima tunic, he's wanted by the SS Gestapo on the south side of Munich.
Traveling on his houseboat to murder victims in Europe, with his buttermilk bicuit batter, butter, and syrup.
Hastening the hogging of hotcakes with a hoot, holler, and howl, a pre-madonna prankster on a proactive prowl.
Crossing the pond to rip innocent bystanders to shreds, he even sneaks in and mauls them in their beds.
All because the swamp mud reacted with moon's reflection of the sun, forming the funky foundation of a fanatical fiend for

felonious fun.

A collusive corporate catastrophe because their red line couldn't budge, forming four-hundred forty-four football fields full of fermenting fudge.

Just spray it with more poison to make the slick sink, they'll think the subterranian cloud is just octopus ink.

Now the deep-sea lightbulb fish will all go blind, making a major mistake and now the milky muck needs mined.

Ocean floor toxic sludge that never goes away, and you know and I know they'll never have to pay.

Ingesting poison transforming angels into tricks and hoes, spoiled brat crybabies blowing their nose.

Serving polluted fishsticks to consumers on a silver platter, mutinous maggots and men who don't matter.

Worthless wealthy worms who waylay the weak, then tell them to shut up when it's their turn to speak.

We heard your manufactured message and it came in clear, you're wallowing in a mudhole of doubt and fear.

You're sitting in a puddle with your hands in the glop, you're a filthy dirtbag and your mouth needs a mop.

Your polluted gullet proclaims what you are, you're stuck in a bottomless pit but you're reaching for a star.

You like steeping on toes and throwing gasoline on fire, abandoning honesty and recommending a liar.

Throwing sound doctrine in the mud because you disagree, denouncing the special provisions our forefathers made for you and me.

You're headed to the fiery furnace of desintegration, as I become the posterchild of a peace-loving nation.

Children on Main Street USA will be overcome with emotion, women will want me to sire their kids on a whimsical notion.

Pilgrims from Rome will visit my boyhood home, bums will be walking by your gravesite puking yellow foam.

The seagull's inland migration will signal the collapse, I'll be surveying the damage and making new maps.

We'll bury you with your bowtie to put your mind at ease, sailors will sing this song to salute your sanctimonious sedition as they sail the seven seas."

The severely inebriated audience was blown away because the jumbotron had a warship sailing through the swamp and the men were ridiculing the traitorous scumbags who made excuses for the evil bastards who thought selling their fellow countrymen and women down the polluted rivers of corporate greed was a winning strategy. They were ripping up photgraphs of TV personalities and sellouts who joined the long list of liars who helped destroy the country they grew to love and it was glorious to say the least. The video went perfectly with the lyrics and the last image was of broken famous faces floating in the murky waters of the swamp. When it was finally over they had to admit it was a masterpiece of artful imagination. They cheered, whistled, and hollered for more as the Chinese Rapper took his final bow.

We made a lot of money that night and my boss was more than happy about it. He came over and patted me on the back for suggesting these boys return to redeem themselves which they obviously did. I got many good tips and the customers were in a good mood after the show with steady customers sticking around until closing time telling stories about the wild performance of the Cinese Rapper. My boss even gave me a big, fat raise for the increase in sales and I was looking forward to paying off some bills and tuition that have been mounting for some time. A lot of folks asked me where we found these boys and I just told them they wandered in one day as I was preparing drinks and asked if there was any way we could hire them for a performance. The rest is history or so they say. He did turn out to be a bad mamma jamma as he always cheesily put it.

CHAPTER 11

It was neat seeing the Chinese Rapper rise to the top, fall back through the cracks, and then pick himself up by the bootstraps to become a formiddable foe to the wicked men who turned their backs on their principles for a few lousy bucks. This little dude ended up redeeming himself through his music like a true artist would do. He played several other gigs at the Shanghai Sushi Lounge and then disappeared from the scene about as fast as he showed up. I turned out to be a big fan of this Chinese crooner and kept the CDs he gave me to play whenever I got bored or was in a nostalgic mood. Some new acts played the venue but none of them rose to the orderinous and aristic display of showmanship which the Chinese Rapper exhibited.

A couple months later I ventured into a local casino to try my luck at the slots and the 21 table when I recognized the Chinese Rapper sitting up at the bar and lo and behold he was sitting next to his cowboy friend, the paid heckler. I approached and shook both their hands and they invited me to sit at a nearby table for a couple drinks and offered to puchase them for me this time.

"I'll be a son of a gun, what are you two boys doing hanging around this joint?" I asked as the waitress took our order.

"Oh, we frequent this place when we're in the area for the loose slots and cheap liquor," replied the cowboy.

"You mean the loose sluts and cheap bicker, don't you Texas boy?" the Chinese Rapper retorted.

"You know what I mean, you Chinese, little weasel."

"You boys can drop the act now, you're not on stage anymore, at least I don't think we are," I mentioned looking around for some kind of camera crew.

"It's cool man, we always act like this, even if we aren't drunk," the cowboy commented chuckling.

"What you talking about? We grew up together on a donkey farm and incorporated our bizarre upbringong into our music. I'm not really from China, I come from the same ranch as this pie-eating goober northeast of Houston, lived there all my life. My daddy was a cook on the ranch and my mama was taken a long time ago leaving my father to raise me the best he knew how," explained the Chinese Rapper.

"That's right, you bartending piece of horse manure. My daddy owned the ranch and employed this kid's father as the cook and we grew up together and made friends even though we act like we want to kill each other half the time. Truth is I wouldn't know what to do without the Chinese Rapper since my daddy died and left me the ranch. My mama died early also and our fathers became inseperable just like we did. They taught us how to sing old country western songs to pass the time away on cattle drives and such," the cowboy said as he was searching his memory banks to recall.

"So why the hell are you guys always cutting down each others' mamas?" I asked not expecting an answer.

"It's just something we always do that seems to ease the pain. It's too hard to think about them and we lost them so early we figure insulting one anothers' mamas was our way of dealing with never having them around and since they're not here to defend themselves the sky's the limit. One thing we would never do is cut down each others' fathers because that would be the ultimate insult that might end up in a life or death battle between two brothers. Now do you understand?" asked the Chinaman.

"I guess so. I have to admit it was pretty funny the way you boys carried on at times but I'll always wonder if the audience was entertained or repulsed by it."

"You know they liked it more than any music ever made since the beginning of time. We rehearsed daily for 15 years before we perfected it enough to make a go at it. Your sushi bar bossman went to school with both of us and he couldn't say no to his old classmates," the Chinese Rapper informed me.

"Yeah man, we made him an offer he had no way to refuse. We told him if he didn't hire us we would burn that sucker to the ground and after some handringing and hardnosed negotiating we ironed out the deal."

"My boss might be a hard ass but he never turns his back on profits so I'm sure you boys earned your keep fairly well or he would've turned you out into the street. I've seen him turn away better acts than you because they didn't appeal to a broader spectrum of fans."

"There is no better act than us. Haven't you figured that out by now? You American, little punk. We've been doing this since before you were born and that's why it comes so natural to us," the Chinese Rapper offered.

"That's right, you city dweller. What in tarnation gives you the right to compare our once in a lifetime performance to other acts who were born with silver spoons where the sun don't shine?" asked the cowboy.

"I didn't mean any disrespect. I was just going to mention that I've seen acts come and go but yours was different. It had a way of appealing to a wider range of fans," I commented trying to backtrack.

"That's not what he said, is it Chinaman? This boy must take us for a couple foolhardy outlaws out to take something we didn't earn the hard way, through manual labor. I bet he told our fans they'd never see us again unless it was in some kind of circus or carnival, when we earned the right to win a grammy," the cowboy said.

"You might have a point there, cowboy. Maybe we ought to take him out to the donkey farm and lynch his sorry ass in the old hanging tree out back so he can join our mamas in the old cow patty in the sky."

"Why you dumbass privileged snots. I was trying to give you some constructive criticism but I can see I made a mistake thinking you idiots had what it takes to make it in the real world. Just go back to the burial places of your ugly and fat mamas and leave the real music to the famous rappers in New York and LA. Those boys have more talent in the pinkies than you mongrels do in your whole bodies. To hell with both you fools and have a nice life training donkeys out there on the farm. I have never in my life seen a couple scoundrels like you who thought it was a good idea to have a hired heckler making cracks and cutting down your own act as a way to garner more support. Maybe if you worked together to provide the fans with a good, solid two or three hours of entertainment you can drop these shenanigans and just sing like everybody else. You did good when you were both on stage dancing and whatnot but this heckling business is weird," I mentioned.

"That's awful rich coming froma weather-beaten windbag such as yourself. Me and this here Chinese boy will tar and feather your ass and run you out of town like the northern revenuer you are. Coming down here busting up moonshine stills and crushing dreams like some kind of Hollywood hotshot. Why don't you go back to where you came from and leave us country folk alone? Don't you have some shows to critique back at that pathetic sushi bar with your fatass boss who doesn't know raw talent when he sees it?"

"Yeah-yeah, you American little punk. Don't you have anything else to do than ruin the careers of two hard working Texans just trying to make it in this cruel rap game. I need to expand my horizons to get my flows recognized by some true-blue media moguls."

"Hey now, wait a New York minute here, I didn't mean to throw cold water on your act or nothing. I just think it might be wise to step up your game and keep on dancing and singing and leave the heckling for the fans if they decide to make fun of your silly asses. Plus, I was born and raised in Texas so I don't understand where you get off calling me a northerner or whatever. I need to get back on the road again, so you boys carry on and don't take everything so personal when someone's just trying to help your ungrateful hides," I answered.

I left them numbskulls crying in their beer about their own

ridiculous presumptions. I damn near forgot about them when one weekend my boss informed me that he gave the duo another gig for that weekend. I kind of rolled my eyes when he announced the show and went outside to add the name of the Chinese Rapper on the neon sign facing the street. When friday finally came around the crowd was huge as word spread about the gig. I was happy with the huge beverage sales but a little apprehensive about what might transpire. As soon as he came out he mentioned the bartending critic sneering at him from the back of the room and the crowd turned and gave me dirty looks. The music started and was a rock-a-billy number with a unique beat that got everyone cheering. My heart kind of sank as he eased into his bizarre lyrics.

Ungrateful Bartender

"What we have here in an ungrateful bartender.
He thinks he's a psychoanalyst and a cool mind bender.
Always criticizing the best rapper you've ever seen.
Coming out to the donkey farm begging for some green.
Proclaiming an untimely demise of the Chinese rapper.
Why don't you try to turn me off by using the clapper?
The cowboy saved my career by giving some advice.
Ignore that dumbass bartender and then do it twice.
He's jealous of the Shanghai Shyster and his crooning.
The next time we see his face our asses will be mooning.
What kind of redneck crowd gets drunk off his drinks? And if you
ask me his boss and his raw sushi stinks.
They won't even serve my favorite, fishheads and rice.
I don't see men in this crowd, just meaningless mice.
Ignoring the revelations of a world-wide psychic.
You deserve a flying roundhouse, face-high sidekick.
To wipe that shit-eating grin off your butt-ugly faces.
For trying to belittle a man bringing together the races.
Black, brown, yellow, the red man and whites.
But they end up in the mosh pit in do-or-die fights.
My bodyguards step in to end the drunken madness.

When you think of my retirement you're overwhelmed with sadness.
I had to grace this place with my intergalactic presence.
To finally see my name in big, bright fluorescence.
My act was ridiculed by the proprietors of this dump.
Trying to beat my royal flush with a four aces trump.
Cheating at the game with hidden cards up his sleeve.
When I leave here tonight the bartender will grieve.
His sugar daddy rapper will leave him in the dust.
So go ahead and honor his ridiculous skills if you must.
Mixing gross drinks that make everybody puke.
He's not a king, or a nobleman, or even a lowly duke."

I just kind of stood there with my mouth agape as he insulted my trade. The crowd didn't respond very well to his confounded foolishness and the audience was mostly silent after this number. He gave me an evil eye that was cold and deadly before retreating backstage as his paid heckler tried to assure the crowd that they haven't seen the last of the Chinese Rapper. The band all looked at each other like they weren't sure what to do and their music kind of wained off as they became convinced he wasn't coming back. A few moments later the cowboy made it back to my bar and asked me to go talk with the disgruntled Chinese rapper to persuade him to finish the act with some of his old songs the crowd always responded well to. I threw down the towel I was using to wipe the counter angrily and followed the heckler cowboy backstage to talk the crazy rapper into singing some more tunes.

"What the hell is going on around here man, why don't you go back out there and finish the show?"

"I demand a heartfelt apology for your criticism of my act."

"I'm the man who should be demanding a damn apology for you cutting down my way of life. I've been mixing these drinks to pay for my college to get a real job after I graduate man, I don't need this silly bullshit in my life right now. You're the one who decided to go out there with some mediocre song about the man who hurt your crybaby feelings when you're supposed to be some king of gangster rapper. What the hell?"

"Fine then, you American little punk! Take your shot glasses and your mixing cauldron and get the hell out of this establishment before I xiung xiu your face."

"Don"t you mean kung fu? Nobody around here ever heard of this xiung xiu crap! You need to take your fish heads and rice on down the road to another venue and quit stinking up this place with this meaningless drivel."

I didn't notice before but the cowboy went to go get my boss as me and the Chinese rapper were arguing and he walked in right as I was telling him off and he fired me right there on the spot. I stormed out of there with the cowboy tagging along behind trying to apologize for the misunderstanding saying he would find a way to smooth things over with my boss. He retreated backstage again after I quit responding and I followed him back there to eavesdrop on the makeshift meeting.

"Your bartender out there is cramping my style and we don't go for that crap back in China. If we were there I'd swash him with a tree of a lumber stick."

"Can't you find someone better than him to mix drinks for the fans hanging on every word of this crazy rapper from China? We showed you respect by coming here to share our beautiful music and we feel we deserve better than that rebellious thug. He made fun of our mamas and told us we didn't have what it takes to make it in the rap scene here in Austin," the cowboy mentioned.

"Calm down boys, you heard how I fired his ass to make you fellas happy, now go out there and finish the show or you won't be getting a dime from me and you damn sure won't be invited back," my boss asserted.

I walked out after hearing these backstabbers. I don't have time to waste trying to spoonfeed wisdom to a couple of gutless cowards who can't even stand up to a little criticism. I sat on the curb out front listening to the Chinese Rapper crying about his green teeth mama and almost laughed at the absurdity of these two weird scoundrels until I realized they cost me my job. The cowboy lied about smoothing things over with my boss just to turn around and make matters worse. I was about to walk back to my car behind the restaurant mad as hell when my boss came out and told me not to assume the worst and take things so literal and that he'd hire me back after the show was over and these two misfits were gone.

"His best songs were the ones I wrote for his silly ass and I don't take too kindly to the way they made the crowd blame me for his ridiculous shenanigans. I made the Chinese Rapper famous and this is the thanks I get."

"Calm down barkeep, you know I appreciate the things you did to introduce this strange phenomenon known as the Chinese Rapper and you did help me sell tons of sushi, so I'm extending your welcome as soon as these boys move on down the road. Just take a short vacation and when you come back things will have calmed down and you can resume bartending as usual and forget you ever met these odd characters."

"Well, I appreciate the offer but maybe my time here is close to expiring anyway. I'll take a vacation and think about it but as far as I'm concerned the Chinese Rapper and his paid heckler can drop off the face of the earth and it wouldn't bother me a bit."

I saw the infamous Chinese Rapper as he exited the building and he flipped me off as my boss turned his back to wave goodbye to the best bartender this dump ever had. I did end up going back to my lucrative job at the Shanghai Sushi Lounge but my heart wasn't in it like it was before I ever set eyes on this Chinese bastard and his bloviated cowboy companion. If you ever see the Chinese Rapper performing at a theatre near you I hope you enjoy his music but just know he's a yellow-belly bastard and a real idiot behind the scenes. Don't fall for the phony facade he exhibits to the public. I do have to admit though that I made a lot of money off this book and was surprised one day when my boss handed me a check for $25,000 for residuals on my copywrited songs I allowed him to perform.

I was at a book signing ceremony in the parking lot behind the Austin City Limits when here comes the Chinese Rapper and his cowboy friend and they were both apologizing heavily and made sure I got the check for the songs. I signed a book after they bought it but gave them the brush-off when they tried to convince me to write some more songs which they offered to pay me handsomely for and they left feeling defeated and deflated of their pomp and glory. It just goes to show some people don't know a good thing when they see one until it's too late to do anything about it. If any true musicians approach me I'd gladly hand them some songs to make their careers just to see the faces of these two fish-eyed fools when they realize they've been had.

Last I heard these boys went back out to the ranch and disappeared off the radar screen. They sure made a good run at it and many folks hated to see the act come to a close even though I have to admit I wasn't one of those. At the height of his career he managed to throw a monkey-wrench into his own potential by incorporating an unproved method of taking his act on the road with a paid heckler to arouse curiosity and draw in a larger array of fans. Several folks asked about him from time to time and I told them he must've fell off the edge of the earth. I witnessed the rise and fall of the Chinese Rapper and they were both glorious and well-deserved.

He came a long way from his Shanghai roots and I later determined he must've edited his portfolio as a way to draw in fans and he probably lied about ever even being in Shanghai where he supposedly started. I don't know what gets into people like him to think about betraying everybody with some made up facts about how he got stated in show biz. I guess it did add a sense of intrigue and mystery to his shadowy beginnings but I no longer check that site for historical verifications.

The End

(Or just the beginning depending on how you look at it)

ABOUT THE AUTHOR

Jeff Crowder

The Chinese Rapper is a book I'm proud of that will hopefully make a splash in the entertainment industry as a token of goodwill to our Chinese counterparts trying to make it in the dangerous and rewarding rap game. If you enjoyed this bizarre novel please check out my other books, such as: Space Junk Pirates, Ricky Road I, II, and III, Swept Under the Carpet, The Honey Tree and the Green Goblin, King Sawbuck, and Miscreated Mania. I think you'll be pleasantly surprised.

www.ingramcontent.com/pod-product-compliance
Lightning Source LLC
Chambersburg PA
CBHW051441150726
48000CB00005B/2191